THE
GRADUAL
DISAPPEARANCE
of
JANE
ASHLAND

"Why did you come back?"

"The power would not be contained any longer. If I had tried to escape it would have destroyed the Worlds; and besides, I understood at last."

"Understood what?"

"Your love for the Worlds and what you would do to save them. And what you would not do. But you have trapped me anyway, for you have taught me to love the Worlds too.

"I do not desire to return to the void and to what I was before, myself and always alone. I will walk into the Heart of the Earth and dream the Worlds until the ages end."

It was becoming hard to breathe now. He looked at her, saw the fire only just concealed behind her human form. She was crying.

"With all the power I have, there is one thing I cannot do, and that is to give back life. I cannot save you."

"It doesn't ..."

"Sssh. Hear me. I cannot save you, but I can give you strength for a few minutes more. Walk into the fire with me Morgan. Walk into the Heart of the Earth. We will become part of everything, together we will dream the Worlds and maybe some small part of each of us will remain. Walk into the fire with me, Morgan. I do not want to dream alone through all the ages of the Worlds."

He lifted a hand to wipe a tear from her face. "I will go into the flames with you."

She bent and put her hand over his wound. He felt warmth flow from it throughout his body and felt some strength return. After a moment Erda took her hand away, but the warmth remained. She helped him to his feet and they stood together looking at the world around them: the wood below, drenched in birdsong, the reflection of the sun on the river, the scent of water and of green things growing.

"We should go now," she said and looking at her he could see that the power could barely be contained by her human form any more. He looked his last on the Wildwood and turned to walk with her into the cave.

The Heart of the Earth burned with heatless light, its fire reflected and redoubled by the walls. The air was cool and fresh.

Morgan looked at Erda, translucent with power. Perhaps this was not an end, but a beginning.

Hand in hand, they walked into the fire and the flames rose about them and they were gone.

Kate and David crept to the front door and looked through the spy hole and into the garden. They stared at each other for a second and bolted for the stairs, Ben trailing in their wake. All the way to the top they ran and pulled open the shutters and found Edinburgh all around them, as it should be, no trace of the battle that had raged moments earlier.

"Did we win? We won the game, didn't we? Didn't we Kate? We won."

"Yes, Ben, we won."

David said quietly, "But how? I wonder what happened."

"Morgan will tell us."

They waited for a long time that day and for many other days, but Morgan did not come.

The Heart of the Earth burned strong and steady but now there were two pinpoints of golden light suspended in it.

Morgan?
Erda?
Yes.

THE
GRADUAL
DISAPPEARANCE
of
JANE
ASHLAND

NICOLAI HOUM

Translated from the Norwegian by Anna Paterson

PUSHKIN PRESS

Pushkin Press
71–75 Shelton Street
London, WC2H 9JQ

The Gradual Disappearance of Jane Ashland was first published as
Jane Ashlands gradvise forsvinning in Norway, 2016

First published by Pushkin Press in 2018

Published by agreement with Copenhagen Literary Agency ApS,
Copenhagen

This translation has been published with the financial support of NORLA

1 3 5 7 9 8 6 4 2

ISBN 13: 978-1-78227-377-6

Author photo © Paal Audestad

Typeset by Tetragon, London
Printed and bound by CPI Group (UK) Ltd, Croydon CR0 4YY

www.pushkinpress.com

For Mother

S HE HAS READ somewhere that this situation usually ends with people taking their clothes off. You get it wrong that final, fatal time and then, there you lie in your underwear, your bluish-white skin stretched tight and your eyeballs frozen solid, time passes and you become covered by a shroud of new snow that has to be gently brushed away by those who find you.

All she can see through the mist is a huge boulder just an arm's length away, and if she leans her head a little to the left, the brightly coloured tent looking like a mouldy orange under its crust of frost.

She shouldn't have lain down. But when she tries to raise her head, she realizes that her hair has got stuck in one of the countless Velcro pads on that state-of-the-art anorak, hugely expensive but still as cold as the heather beneath her, and she cannot find the energy to do anything about it.

Now, while she is still conscious, she must lock her fingers in a dramatic pose.

Oh my God, it looks as if she tried to grab at something at the moment of death!

And the rescuers will avert their heads in distaste. Someone in the team will break the arm so that the theatrical gesture won't be in the way when the corpse is fitted into the bag tied to some kind of stretcher or sledge so that it can be hauled down the hill.

What should she reach for, how should she make it look?

S HE HAD BEEN GIVEN so much alcohol and legroom in the plane she felt like a ragdoll left by a child in a massive armchair. They must be upgrading people to business class whenever there's some hassle about the ticket. The guy next to her had presumably also drawn a winning number; both of them looked out of place among all the white shirts. She wore jeans and a college sweater and he, a red checked flannel shirt and hiking boots. So, here we are, she thought. And then felt uncertain if she'd actually said it out loud, because he quickly turned to her and smiled.

'It wasn't anything.'

'What?'

She focused on the handbag she still had on her lap, disappeared into it like an animal digging for something. She had noticed him in the departure lounge. Thick blond hair, even though he was nearer fifty than forty. Neatly trimmed beard. Eyes so blue they might have been for decorative effect. He could easily have been the unknown fifth member of ABBA. Not her type. Though she wasn't convinced she had a type.

She emerged from the handbag with a blister pack, twisted round to face the window and swallowed ten milligrams of

Valium without water. Three baggage handlers were heaving suitcases into the hold through some hatch she couldn't see.

'Not keen on flying?' he asked.

She didn't reply and the expectation of her saying something contracted like the field of vision before a fit, growing smaller and smaller until it became as uninteresting as the noises in the cabin. Suddenly, there were clouds outside just where the men had been moving about on the rain-soaked tarmac. Dr Rice would have called it a hypnagogic state. A microsleep. A stewardess stopped at their row of seats. She asked for a whisky and a Coke.

As she leant across him to take the glass, the can of Coke and the small bottle of alcohol, she noticed him glancing down at her breasts and, in these few seconds, enjoyed the sensation of remembering something so remote she had forgotten to miss it.

'My name is Ulf, if you want to know,' the man in the next seat said.

'Is that a real name?' she asked.

She finished her drink while he told her that he was on his way home from Nunavut in Canada after completing a two-year-long research project on the herding behaviour of the musk ox. Once upon a time this would definitely have interested her; life had provided ideas for new short stories or novels, and people she met became models for fictional characters. Asking follow-up questions had become a habit. Her subjects usually grew fascinated by her eagerness to learn. Her questioning made her seem intelligent. Did you fly from Iqaluit? That part of her brain was still active and functioned independently, like clockwork without hands to move.

'What about you?' he asked. When he spoke, with what she assumed was a Scandinavian accent, the words came out loud and clear between his strong, white teeth.

She raised her eyes over the top of the seats, with their little white cloth squares placed there to catch businessmen's dandruff, and looked for the stewardess with the drinks trolley. Then, she said that she wanted to connect with her roots.

'I've spent some time on investigating my family origins.'

The phrase *spent some time on* sounded better than *been totally fucking obsessed by*. Just like clearing out the house, or like that online lecture she got so deep into.

After she had let him know that she came from Wisconsin, he said, 'I assume you've heard about the Wisconsin glaciation?'

She shook her head. It was too difficult to work out whether he was irritating or charming. He had commandeered the armrest between their seats.

'The Wisconsin Glacial Episode? Some 70,000 years ago?' he went on.

'It doesn't ring any bells, I'm afraid. But it was rather long ago.'

He clearly didn't find that amusing, and simply said, 'Anyway, back in those days, there were musk oxen around in your home state.'

The stewardess with the drinks went off in the wrong direction.

'And now you're planning to visit your relatives?'

She tipped the last of the half-moon-shaped bits of ice from the bottom of her plastic cup into her mouth and, with her mouth full to sound more casual, said, 'I needed to get away for a while.'

She bent forward, her head between her knees, placed the now empty cup on the carpet, and pulled the neck of a bottle of Southern Comfort out of her bag. And drank, straight from the bag, as if it had been one of these old-style hiking bottles.

'The Inuit have this expression...' Ulf stared straight ahead when he said this, chortled and drew his lips back, letting his row of large, white teeth light up his surroundings, 'If you're afraid, walk in a new direction.'

'Here's another one' she said. 'When the snow melts, you'll see the dog shit.'

Halfway across the Atlantic, when the stewardess would no longer respond when she pressed the button, she slumped in her seat, wishing that the man next to her was not asleep. She could hear his breathing. For a while, his eyelids trembled. Once they were still again, a narrow, white slit was still showing between his eyelashes, almost as if he were awake.

'As a biologist...' she began to address him in her thoughts. Naturally, he corrected her: 'Zoologist'. She rolled her eyes at that and carried on with her imaginary account of the lecture she had watched online. With his training and experience, could Ulf please make sense of these ideas?

'You see, this famous physicist was speaking about how, among scientists, there is a growing acceptance of the notion that there's something more than this life, than our world. Well, it's not as simple...'

'But a greater consciousness?' he said, meaning to be helpful. 'Something that is external to us, or is greater than any one individual? A dimension we don't know about?'

'Exactly. And might there be something in it?'

'Yes, absolutely. It cannot be denied. By the way, you're amazingly attractive. You still look great.'

'Thank you.'

'If you like, lean on me and rest your head on my shoulder. Just to feel the warmth of my body. No commitments.'

So, she allowed her hand to slide along the armrest until it touched his, pressed closer to the large, sleeping body and pretended that she, too, was asleep.

S HE HAS A WATCH. She is pretty sure it has been three days and nights so far. Sun goes up, sun goes down. The so-called comfort temperature of the sleeping bag is said to be six degrees centigrade but, as of now, there's nothing comfortable about it. The sulphurous haze of fog is still as dense and someone up there is playing with the on-off switch for the wind. Abruptly, the tent becomes a perfect dome again and all she can hear is the pale-grey hum she has come to think of as the sound of the mountains.

He took the map when he left. Her mobile is out of juice. The only edible thing in the tent is mackerel in tomato sauce and barely half of it is left in the tin no bigger than a deck of cards. The contents have a fishy, bluish shine and taste metallic, like chunks of the actual trawler.

She needs to drink. With the sleeping bag bunched up around her waist, she crawls to the front of the tent. Once the zip is pulled halfway down, a shower of freezing rain slaps her in the face. She wriggles out of her sleeping bag, puts her boots on and, stooping, emerges into all that whiteness.

Beyond that stone begins the territory you must keep out of. Over there, the negative force can get you. That is why you have to stay on this side of the stone. Stick to the area between the tent and the stone, right? Then the puddle of water is on the borderline, kind of.

If I've got that right, then drinking the near-side water is fine?

Yes, only not from the other side. That won't do.

She kneels down, as if in prayer, in front of the small, reflecting surface and looks into her own wild eyes for a brief moment before her chin breaks up the mirror image. As she straightens her back and swallows like a long-necked bird, she recalls something Hemingway is supposed to have said: *Never go on trips with anyone you do not love.*

But, then, Hemingway also said: *Madame, all stories, if continued far enough, end in death…*

'**E**XCUSE ME, you really must speak up.'
(…)

'Could you possibly raise your voice, Ms. Ashland?'
(…)

'I'm sorry. It's just that you're mostly inaudible.'
(…)

'I realize that, in your mind, the sound of our voice is coming out clearly but that is not actually the case.'
(…)

'The prosecution should postpone the hearing until the witness is capable of making her statement. I would have appreciated if assurances had been obtained in good time that Ms. Ashland was…'
(…)

'Ms. Ashland, I must ask you to let go of the microphone and leave the witness stand now.'
(…)

'Ms. Ashland? You can…'
(…)

'Jane Ashland?'

A T FIRST, you will feel that constructing a wall is essential, Dr Rice had told her. A wall between yourself and all the insensitive comments made by your friends, family and acquaintances who either ought to know better, or else are simply unable to understand.

Her parents were quickly sent to the far side of that wall. Not because they said so many fatuous things – that is, apart from her mother, who kept using the term 'accident' in her whispering tone of voice, one of the critical factors in Jane's decision to leave home at the age of eighteen – but because they, unlike herself, seemed to have kept the cores of their being intact. Unlike her, they had not become fearless. They never failed to lock the front door, never stopped strapping themselves into safety belts. Nor did they consistently choose to sleep on the sofa instead of in bed. They did not break plates. For them, day-to-day existence did not alternate between strict adherence to routine and being utterly adrift, without a sense of time. She didn't think they were urging Dr Rice, or anyone else, to prescribe more and more tablets for them. As far as she knew, they sought sanctuary neither in the shower nor in the car, the only places nowadays where people can scream out loud or wail wordlessly.

True, her parents moved house. Into an apartment in a new housing development, some twenty-five miles from what had been Jane's childhood home. The development consisted of identical rows of apartment blocks surrounded by a landscaped area rather like a golf course. There was an artificial canal crossed by a small arched bridge. Her dad had tried to catch catfish from the bridge but gave up after being soaked several times by the automatic sprinklers. They had new furniture held together with screws that forever needed tightening, and a complicated air-conditioning system that demanded much attention from her father. Jane's mother had changed their favourite old armchair for a red wine-coloured La-Z-Boy. Sitting in it, looking out through the bay window, Dorothy had a view free from memories. The window occasionally annoyed them, though, because it didn't face the lake as the agent had assured them it would.

Jane went to visit her parents three days before her departure. She had put on make-up. Fixed her hair. Her clothes were clean. Only her timing was wrong.

'I thought it might be you,' her father said as he opened the door. His eyes were mere slits, and he was in his dressing gown. Her mother, who immediately started making pancakes, insisted they been up and about for hours and tried to block the view of the clock on the stove. It showed 05.15.

'Are you sure you'll want to go travelling?' she asked, keeping her back turned.

Jane didn't have to reply.

'Of course she's sure, Dorothy. She bought the tickets, didn't she?'

'Well, you know best, Robert.'

'You may call me Bob,' he said. 'After all, we've been married for almost fifty years.'

After breakfast, they left Dorothy in the chair by the window and took the lift to the ground floor. The sun had just risen. Jane had left her car with the trunk gaping open like a metal monster, digesting after having swallowed the remains of her life: cardboard boxes, a Fisher-Price castle, a yellowed computer monitor. How far away had she been when she selected these things to keep?

Neither of them made a move towards unloading the car. They just stood in the dazzling, diffuse morning light, arms crossed. Then, her father astonished her with a nakedly emotional outburst, something he rarely permitted himself and normally didn't seem to need. He clenched his jaw, shut his eyes tightly and pointed to his chest as if describing a site of physical pain.

'It hurts so much, Jane.'

She should have said something then, perhaps hugged him, but somehow did not get it together.

'I regret all the things I didn't do. I have had such an eternity of time on my hands. Dorothy and I, both. I cannot think now why we didn't... take part much more.'

She just nodded.

'Anyway, is it all right if I leave all this?' she asked.

Her father swallowed.

'Yes, of course. We still have the attic space.'

'True, but somehow you...'

The high, thin pitch of their voices hardly carried and meanwhile other sounds seemed muffled, as if the world around them transmitted poorly.

'What will you do about the car?' Her father's shoulders had sagged suddenly.

'I intend to dump it in a wood near the airport and walk the last bit,' she said.

Her father breathed audibly through his nose and looked away.

'What, are you saying I should set fire to it as well?'

Flocks of ring-billed gulls, blown in from Lake Michigan during the night, drifted about as if baffled by the large expanses of grass. Not a soul in sight, even though it was no longer too early in the morning for retired folk.

'Tom wanted the car,' she finally said.

'Tommy Belotti? That greaseball?'

Was her dad the kind of guy who said things like that or did he just make out that he was a guy who said these things? She had never worked this out. He had started on the floor at Pabst but risen swiftly through the ranks to brewing supervisor. Before his twenty-fourth birthday, he was already head of logistics for the East Coast, Midwest and Canada (as he had reminded Jane when she was the same age and had not yet completed her literature degree). For his entire adult life, he had lived in dense suburbs populated by sales people, small-time company directors and middle-management types. His wife read Walt Whitman in bed and had once, in the seventies, collected a substantial sum in support of the new ballet theatre in Milwaukee. His daughter had gone in for literature full-time, a choice he had not tried to talk her out of but had not encouraged either.

'Tommy Belotti has always been after you,' her father said.

'Just in junior high.'

He nodded, still unconvinced.

'How much is he paying you for the car?'

She knew what would come next. Her dad would bend over, seemingly to check the car's chassis and meanwhile get into a state because she was giving away a car in perfectly reasonable condition. So she picked a sum at random.

'Five thousand.'

It was apparently too much. He started rocking on his heels.

'Hello, big spender. Smart move, Belotti.'

'I'm pretty sure Tom's feelings for me had faded by eighth grade. When I got my braces. Thereabouts. At least by the time he was best man at my wedding.'

'Was he?' her father asked.

'Have you forgotten?'

THE ARRIVALS HALL with its furnishings of smooth, hygienic steel and aura of clinical severity had the atmosphere of a detention cell. She had either taken a wrong turning or purposely let herself be diverted through the duty-free shop. Ulf was waiting by the baggage carousel.

'You again,' he said cheerfully.

She stared at the cases that emerged one after the other from underground, and then toppled over onto a new conveyor belt.

'You slept on my shoulder last night, I believe.'

It had to happen. And in the most straightforward way. If this had been Greg, he would surely have said something funny about dribble on his shirt. They would have laughed together. And gone to bed, and lived the rest of their lives together.

'I'm so sorry,' she said.

She noticed him glancing at her again while they waited for their luggage. She considered her appearance from the point of view of a forty-something scientist. A large, straight nose. A rather more golden skin tone than her Scandinavian genes would have generated. Lips that were well-drawn examples of their kind. She would never, unlike most of Ulf's recent conquests, end up with unkissable, bright red lines surrounded by powder. Shoulder-length, nut-brown hair (clever colouring). Her behind filled out her mom jeans nicely but nobody would have classified it as fat, surely, or what was the definition of 'fat'? And what about her breasts, were they for real? he would ask himself. What did they look like without a bra? He would imagine standing behind her in a clean and brightly lit Scandinavian hotel bathroom, watching her in the mirror while she brushed her teeth, and then putting his arms round her, full of a sense of possession, despite not really knowing her. This feeling sustained him and usually compensated him for not falling head over heels in love any more. She looked up at him and smiled compassionately. He misunderstood the smile.

'Look, I like you. And I think that you are… going through something.'

A glint from his massive diver's watch as he pushed his hand through his hair where a boyish, almost white tuft kept sticking straight up. He aroused the same emotions as the countless jocks in her past. She wanted to bite his arm.

'I know how lonely one can feel sometimes, believe you me. I've lived in a trapper cabin for ten months.'

She smiled sardonically but thought: he cannot have a clue how insensitive that comment is.

'What about a cup of coffee?'

'No.'

'Then why not make a note of my telephone number anyway? Then you'll have a friend to contact here. Just in case.'

It seemed easier to do as he said. They stood silently side by side for several minutes, waiting for their luggage.

D R RICE SAID that there had been no *change in the grieving process*. There should be a *change in the grieving process* after six to twelve months. It is a cause for concern if, after six to twelve months, there is no *change in the grieving process*. All this, according to Dr Rice.

In other words, it is generally accepted that grief should show orderly progress.

'Now, what are your thoughts about this?'

'I don't think about it. I haven't set myself any goals.'

'I was under the impression that we had, together?'

'Maybe we did.'

'We have discussed the lifelong outcomes.'

Dr Rice balanced the lifelong outcomes on the palm of his hand.

'That's not, however, what I am talking about now,' he said, and reached out with his other hand. His movements were swift and unusually engaged for someone of his age. 'I'm referring to not seeing any step change, however small, in the short term. I might also consider reducing your medication.'

'"Also"?'

'That's right.'

'Also… what?'

'Jane, I don't weigh every word.'

His eyes were bright and quick, and surrounded by dry, wrinkly skin like a parrot's. Sometimes, she felt she was there mostly to please him.

'For as long as your mind is dulled in various ways, it will be difficult for you to move on, all the way from denial to acceptance.'

'That's the Kübler-Ross model again, right?'

Dr Rice's smile was that of a grandfather having to cope with a troublesome grandchild. She actually felt bad about tormenting him, but the discomfort it caused was as simple and unmistakable as holding one's hand in scalding water. In her previous session with Dr Rice, she had talked about the widespread and growing scepticism towards Elisabeth Kübler-Ross's theoretical stages of grieving, a paradigm that had dominated work with the bereaved for the last forty years. She had also referred to some of the critical articles that, a decade or so after Kübler-Ross's death, described her as a New Age spiritualist and a charlatan whose theory was based on anecdotal observations.

'So good to hear that you find the energy to read, Jane,' Dr Rice had replied, quite without sarcasm.

His office smelt of tear-stained paper tissues. His creaking leather chair allowed him to swing forward and back as he spoke. The room had a window, but looking into what could be another room, or a corridor, because one could sometimes see shadowy figures pass by on the other side of its milky glass. There were no diplomas on the wall above his dry, bald head, but instead framed children's drawings. She had a feeling that during one of her early consultations, he had spoken about his voluntary work with Somalian refugee children, including trauma management.

While he thought, Dr Rice was breathing heavily and loudly through his nose. 'It also seems true to say that the pills don't help to prevent your functional episodes – is that right?'

The word *functional* made Jane think of space-saving wardrobe solutions.

'But, do we still believe that I want to have these episodes?'

'I don't think people in your situation want either one thing or the other. It is all about loss of control. Or, wanting to lose control.'

He turned and looked at the opaque window. His expression suggested a man allowing magnificent scenery to inspire new lines of thought.

'Why don't you write, Jane? Why not start writing again?' She saw his rosy ideas about the author's vocation reflected in his face. 'After all, many have felt that writing has a therapeutic effect. And for you, it is also a profession. I see patients at your stage who simply cling to their work and find that it helps them.'

She didn't have the strength to explain her problem. Once, back in 2003 or perhaps 2004, Jane's editor had sent her a copy of a travelogue called *Stranger on a Train* by the British writer Jenny Diski. *Because you think alike*, it said on the Post-it note that fell out of the bubble wrap envelope. In an especially memorable passage, Diski described her last conversation with a dying friend. When Jane reread that passage recently, it had seemed to express the reason why she no longer wrote: *The nonsense of language reaching towards the void it was not equipped for, developed as it was by the living for the living, made us laugh.*

To make Dr Rice's forehead smoother, she told him instead about her travelling plans. It felt as if she had held back from telling him to achieve the maximum effect.

'Now Jane, this is…' Dr Rice gave the thumbs up, boyishly. He couldn't help himself. That was how his old hand would still show enthusiasm, and one of the few things in this world that were still beautiful.

'That changes everything,' Dr Rice said. 'It points to what I said earlier about initiative and change. I'm biting my tongue, Jane. Norway! Now, I imagine that's a chilly country, Jane! Just how cold, I wonder? Come on, tell me, how cold can it get?'

S HE IS SHIVERING where she lies, fully clothed, inside the sleeping bag, and watches the world outside the tent. The wind has died down, she notes, but the fog is still there. It covers the ground – and she still can't avoid evaluating nature in literary images – like a thick rug.

She misses chiding her college students for using that kind of worn-out simile. Correcting them but making them feel valued at the same time, allowing their youthful, hopeful minds to believe that every one of them is a unique individual and their world will be truly different from that of their parents.

A thick rug on the ground? But of course, writing about nature is actually impossible. One never writes about nature but about various cultural perceptions of it. To speak about it at all, just to name its parts, turns nature into something it is not.

She thinks back to all the rebellious young men she has taught over the years – there was at least one in each class. Why did she let herself be provoked by them? After all, they kept writing, these young men, which demonstrated their belief that the human talent for language could capture all the most terrible, most saddening phenomena on Earth. Deep down, they were optimists, not misanthropists. Their texts investigated immorality, breaches of norms but never reached rock bottom: the place where concepts do not exist.

When you begin to think that your writing is no more than a construction you use to say something about another lot of constructions, and that, meanwhile, the most profound truths of the human condition are forever beyond your reach – then you stop writing. You resign from your post teaching creative writing in the Department of English at the University of Wisconsin at Madison. Your farewell address to the Faculty of Arts makes your colleagues look down at their casual shoes and exchange discreetly supportive glances. Afterwards, they address you with raised eyebrows and in far-too-bright voices: 'Thank you, Jane. That was so good.' You have to take on board that the only two people in the audience who have grasped anything of what you said are José Pérez, who teaches in the Department of Philosophy and Religious Studies, and Art Wilder, who is something in Accounts. Art's wife tried out tandem parachuting in Niagara Falls in 1992 and died in an accident while Art, who had stayed safely on the ground, was watching. You realized this when Art got up and left in the middle of your address. And José comes up afterwards, takes your hand, holds it between both his and says, 'My god, Jane. I know how you feel. Theoretically.'

Then, you take up genealogy. You travel to Norway.

The first nights in Norway, she stayed in a motel room that reminded her of motel rooms back home, apart from all the wood panelling. Before resigning from her university post, she prepared a final handout for the creative writing students, which included extracts from two Scandinavian novels in translation. It so happened that both pieces contained passages in which the protagonist is lying on his back observing knots in the wooden ceiling panels. It seemed a pleasant, meditative thing to do. Thus art improves on reality.

Still, the motel room provided nice physical containment. An electric radiator next to her bed gave off a faint smell of the past being burnt. She had a plastic bag full of provisions. The food was all alien; none of the packaging aroused memories, there were no preferred brands, no favourite chocolate bars. The hire car she had picked up at the airport was parked in front of her door. She had been in touch with the family who, as far as she knew, were some of her closest relatives in Norway, and told them that she would like a couple of days in Oslo to acclimatize. *Visit the Opera House, for instance.* In the end, all she did was speed through the capital city without really noticing it – or, not so much 'through' as 'underneath', inside a gloomy system of tunnels. Once out of the tunnels, she drove on for another half-hour before checking in at the motel. After settling in, she started smoking again (her last cigarette had been twelve years ago), drank exceptionally expensive beer and prepared instant noodles with a small kettle on the dressing table. She found it possible to bear watching TV, even American reality shows that hadn't been dubbed, and no longer looked out for signs or coded messages in the programmes. But she still could not sleep; if she drifted off, it rarely lasted for more than a few minutes at a time.

One morning, her mobile rang. She staggered in her large Snoopy sweatshirt over to her bag and, before answering, said her name out loud twice to make sure she wouldn't sound utterly unhinged. The caller was Lars Christian Askeland-Nilsen.

'There you are! Great!' He seemed to be reading his English sentences off a list.

'Do you really think so?'

'Of course.'

It was just that insecurity of hers that made her spend her first days in Norway alone. She had been looking forward to meeting her long-lost relatives but had begun to doubt if the invitation to stay with them was genuinely meant. Perhaps he had simply urged her to visit the country in general? Perhaps she had introduced the idea of staying with them and Lars Christian had simply affirmed it would be all right? Or perhaps he had just come out with one of these weird Norwegian *hrump* noises, meaning roughly *I'm hearing you*?

In the background, she picked out what must be Eva's voice and another that probably belonged to their daughter Camilla. Lars Christian said that their son Martin was away at summer camp.

'Wow, summer camp.'

'Yes, he's growing up so fast.'

'That's so true,' Jane said, as if she had followed the lad's growth from the sidelines for years. She wasn't even sure there was a word that described their relationship.

As it happened, she had driven quite a long way past their area. They agreed that she would return to the highway and drive back towards Oslo. At a certain exit ramp she was to turn off and stop at a parking lot by the side of the road.

While she waited in the car, she pondered the reaction her Norwegian relatives would expect from her when they met for the first time. Would it strike the right note to do a full, shrieking outburst of joy, American-style? Only last night, she had observed three of these on the TLC channel, though the happiness turned into childish pouting when one of the participants failed to find the wedding dress of her dreams.

She had started with genealogy, mostly because she wanted to have something to tell Dr Rice and others who cared to ask.

I thought I ought to find out about my roots. It feels important at this point in time.

To her surprise, no one seemed surprised. It was a fact that, unlike most of her childhood friends, she had never bothered turning up in Stoughton for the 17th May procession on Norway's national day. She had never been to Little Norway before it closed, hadn't even owned a coffee mug inscribed *Uff da!* Generally, concern about biological origins wasn't her thing. She was Writer-Jane, the intellectual among them. Fundamentally, she had decided that the all-American worship of family history was fascistoid. Once, at a dinner party, she had ended up in a heated discussion on the subject: a friend had several times used the words *pure bloodline* to describe her links to the old country in Europe. It didn't help that the country was Germany.

All the same, she had become hooked the moment she opened *MyHeritage.com* and clicked the *Start* button. She sat in front of the screen for days on end. As the blank fields in her family tree gradually became populated, the growing orderliness felt good. She dug out the histories of her distant relatives in cuttings libraries and registers, and found that they had the grand, inclusive sweep of novels, which she missed being able to write. Rooting around in digitized records and parish documents constantly reminded her that death, viewed from far enough away, amounts to no more than faded ink on dry paper.

For some time before she set out on the journey, she had been exchanging emails with unknown, reserved Norwegians, who were typically better schooled in the English language than her undergraduates. It was a liberating kind of correspondence. The recipients of her queries knew nothing about her other than fragments of distant family relationships:

'It would seem to indicate that either my grandfather or my great-grandfather changed his name from Askeland to Ashland. Also, it confirms that Hjertrud Askeland, whose descendants live in Salinas, have nothing to do with this matter. I feel we have reached a conclusion and can only reiterate that I am very grateful for...'

Lars Christian Askeland-Nilsen had seemed really fascinated by her project. Unasked, he had searched the collection *Letters from America*, held in the National Library in Oslo, and found correspondence between the man who begat Jane's branch of the family and the people he had left behind in Norway. Lars Christian translated extracts from these letters and sent them to her. She googled him and discovered pictures taken at a cross-country run: his running shorts were tight and shiny and his smiling face was splattered with mud.

But the brutality described in the translated letters was hard to take.

'I had no idea that malaria was so prevalent in Texas at the time. Not to mention the Indians,' Lars Christian commented.

Three of Fredrik Melchior Askeland's letters from the middle of the nineteenth century were left. In them, he listed the five children that he and his wife had lost; the youngest was just seven months old. The references to their deaths were made with the absolute minimum of emotion, and interspersed with notes on the weather and accounts of the autumn harvests – so-and-so many barrels of rye and bushels of corn, and I have to tell you that little Martha was taken from us this past August.

'This F.M. Askeland, what is his problem? His wife doesn't seem too bothered either. The children's mother!' Jane wrote in an excitable email.

'I have come to think that the reason is their very strong belief in God,' Lars Christian wrote in reply. 'They profoundly believe that they will meet their children again.'

She had liked his answer. She imagined Lars Christian writing to her while wearing his tiny, shiny shorts. The more they wrote to each other – it was a huge number of messages, though she began to wonder if she hadn't sent many more than she had received – the stronger her wish to go to Norway became. Lars Christian had uploaded pictures of family skiing trips, apparently in perpetual sunshine. She imagined being with them in the pictures.

*

She hesitated with her hand on the door handle, then inhaled deeply, left the car and went to meet the Askeland-Nilsen family. The ground was scattered with wet leaves. The rumbling high-way traffic drowned her too-early 'Hi'.

The daughter hung back behind her father. Her mother stepped forward.

'Jane?'

They shook hands. The fourteen-year-old, too. Her hand was warm, slightly moist, and she kept glancing at her father.

'Any moment now, I'll start looking for family characteristics,' Jane said with a laugh as she scanned each one of them. It wasn't her true reason. All three seemed to have dressed for a moderately severe hike. The morning mist had left drops clinging to their pale eyebrows and trickling down the synthetic material of their anoraks.

It wasn't Lars Christian but Eva, his wife, who took the lead. 'You must be tired. Have you had breakfast?' Her hands moved about like little birds as she spoke.

Lars Christian's light voice interjected with scraps of information that were more or less irrelevant. 'If you'd like a cup of coffee, we've got some cake at home.'

'President Obama had a tough time the other day!'

'Camilla has looked forward so much to showing you our new house.'

The girl stood straight-backed, her eyes following the talk. All three of them were beautiful. They could have been sports stars, of the nice polite kind that answer the TV interviewer's questions factually. Long-distance runners, for instance. Lars Christian's face was so narrow, with crisply defined features, that the skin seemed loose here and there. Eva was just as slim, which gave her a youthful look. Her hairstyle was practical, her face freckled and her eyelashes so pale they were almost invisible. Their daughter was long-limbed and innocent: she made Jane think of perfect, green apples in a new, transparent plastic bag. Suddenly, she regretted not having hugged them all while there was still a faint chance. If only she could leave the hire car behind, join them in their Volvo and sit in the back next to the shy teenager and pick up faint traces of the family's smell in her nostrils.

T HE IDEA HAD BEEN to camp just inside the boundary of a national park and use it as a base for observing the herd of musk oxen, just like everybody else did: safari tours were laid on, there were authorized guides and sets of guidelines about the recommended safe distances – all that is required for potential encounters between large wild animals and modern people. But the day they arrived at the reserve, she in charge of the rucksack and Ulf of four aluminium boxes the size of coffins, the musk oxen had moved northwards. It meant that they had to drop Ulf's plan to drive his all-terrain vehicle along the gravelled tracks that had been cleared by the Norwegian army during the time when the area had been used for ordnance training. Instead they had to prepare to proceed on foot. At first, she thought it was a good thing.

'It's all happening,' Ulf muttered while they redid the packing, leaving the heaviest equipment behind in a shed near the railway track at an outpost called Hjerkinn. The air around them seemed to radiate darkness. What little she could see of the surroundings looked like nothing she had seen before – the erratic beams of the head torches fell on stacks of tar-coated timber, abandoned construction machinery, piles of gravel and stunted trees, bent and twisted by the wind. It didn't look like a place meant for people.

Ulf led the way past a station building, older than the birth of railways by the looks of things. He walked three paces ahead of her, staring at his mobile phone, which he had used all day to stay in touch with local contacts who had suggestions about where to find the musk oxen. A few minutes later, they arrived at a building that had an outdoor lamp spreading a feeble light. Ulf unlocked a door and went inside.

'Where are we?' she asked once she had wrenched the rucksack through the doorway.

'The wild reindeer centre,' Ulf mumbled.

He crossed the room and found the light switch. They were in a large hall with yellowish wall panelling and a staircase painted moss-green. Ulf walked upstairs and waved at her to follow. Given how far they had gone into the wilderness, the first floor was absurdly modern – all glass partitions, name plates, computers. Ulf rolled out a camping mattress on the smooth carpet.

'We'll start walking at sunrise,' he said, a taciturn Red Indian in the middle of an office landscape.

'Do you think we'll find them?'

He stroked her cheek and the gesture seemed simply reassuring.

'Yes, I do. And the territorial groups are due to join up, which is precisely what we have come here to observe.'

She reflected on Ulf's tendency to make technical observations and assume that she would know what he was on about. The conclusion must presumably be that he was an absent-minded professional nerd as well as, maybe, a fascinating lone wolf. So far, they had spent only one and a half days together.

When she phoned him at four-thirty one morning, she had been sitting in the hire car in front of the Askeland-Nilsens' house. This moment, she had felt, was the nadir of her life. As the dawn lightened the air above the Oslo fjord, turning the world an insubstantial shade of grey, she sensed the weight of all she had drunk the day before, and all she had said and done. Ulf offered her a final option, her very last way out. She imagined Ulf as he had been. On the plane. The way he had looked at her when he thought she wouldn't notice. She wanted to let herself topple over backwards and find herself supported.

Whatever. Things could not get any worse.

'Do you remember saying something about *a friend in Norway*?'

There was no need to say anything else. She escaped further humiliation.

'Can you manage to drive to Dombås?' His voice was just as pleasant as she had remembered it.

'Where is that?' she asked.

'Follow the E6.'

'Are you sure?'

'About how to get here?'

She thought he was trying to be funny and smiled with tears running down her cheeks.

On the way up the valley, she experienced the familiar feeling of having just learnt how to breathe, and that it was something she still needed to practise. As the day grew brighter and the sky bluer, her sense of alienation increased. She stopped a couple of times, climbed out of the car to take in yet another beautiful view, finding everything dizzyingly unreal. What was she doing here? Why was she standing in this place, alone, next to a car that wasn't hers, just off a road she didn't know in a country she had never been to before and staring out into its landscape? Had she really spoken with Ulf on the phone or imagined it?

He hugged her when she arrived. She leant her head against his chest and tried to make herself stop sobbing.

'It will work out. Surely you remember that Inuit saying?'

Realizing how good it felt to be held by him, she suppressed the heightened sense of strangeness that came with his smell, his hands resting on her back.

Ulf was staying in a run-down motel, a wooden one-storey shack, once painted red. It had a reception area at one end. Every room had its own small terrace furnished with two plastic chairs and a plastic table with an ashtray on it. On Ulf's table, there was also a dead pansy in a white pot marked *Grand Jardin des Fleurs*.

The evening was exceptionally mild for Norway in October, or so Ulf said. They settled on the terrace and started drinking beer – she drained the first glass in one go, as if she had just crossed a desert.

She told Ulf everything. She soon found herself using technical narrative devices and had little pangs of nausea every time she gave her story a touch of foreshadowing or a new plot twist. Ulf chewed nuts from a bag of chilli-flavoured peanuts, and grinned towards the sun that warmed them. He put his head empathetically to the side as he listened and said 'oh, no' or 'yes, I see' or 'I see what you mean'. His beard wasn't as neatly trimmed as it had been before. He wore glasses, which he hadn't done on the plane, with frames made of transparent, bright-red plastic of the kind one might buy in order to look young but which no young person would have bought.

When she had concluded the last chapter in the tale of her five days in the house of the Askeland-Nilsens, Ulf asked, 'So, you just left?'

'I sneaked outside and set off down the drive.'

'Why not tell them the truth?'

She shrugged and raised part of her upper lip, then realized how many of her youthful facial expressions had come back during the last six months or so.

'Because you wanted to make a fresh start,' Ulf went on. It was a statement, not a question.

But it hadn't been that simple.

'I didn't want to end up being angry with them. And didn't want to place them in a situation in which they'd be bound to say something idiotic.'

'Like what?'

'*How are you?* for instance.'

Ulf grabbed a handful of nuts and his forehead creased.

'Or, even worse: *You're so strong, I wouldn't have been able to carry on,*' she added.

The hand that was transferring the nuts to his mouth stopped halfway.

'Did you contact them today, after you left?'

'Goodness, no.'

'But won't they wonder where you are?'

'Shouldn't think so.'

'So, they haven't even called to find out how you are?'

'No. I've only had one call. It was the car hire people, who wanted to know how long I wanted to keep the car for.'

Ulf's lips moved as she spoke. It made for an oddly intimate impression. She really appreciated the way he hadn't made a big performance about how eccentric it was to drive a whole day in order to pour out your life story to a man you had only met once and had nearly snubbed. It spoke well of his character, somehow.

'What do you think the girl is feeling?'

'I think the entire family is relieved that I left.'

'Did you feel sad?'

'*Feel sad*?'

Her tone of voice suggested that *feeling sad* was simply pathetic.

'Ill at ease?'

'If I did, it would have been an entirely natural emotional response to the situation.'

The sentence was problematic. Sitting at the table, she occupied more space now. Her mouth had become broader. She had lost track of how much she had drunk. And how many tablets she had taken.

The view from Ulf's terrace could have been magnificent if it hadn't been for the building that stood in the way. It had apparently been erected in the same joyless spirit as the motel. The windows were boarded over and the text on the wall said *Dombås Cinema*. The ridge of its roof was almost exactly level with the tops of the mountains.

Ulf flicked the last nut into his mouth.

'I shall have to go up into the mountains tomorrow.'

He nodded in the general direction of the tall pickup truck that was parked in the yard in front of the motel. There was a snow scooter on the truck's trailer and the ATV as well, squeezed in between jerrycans and large boxes.

'How long will you be away for?'

The question sounded intrusive but he replied, 'I figured you might like to come along. Sleep in a tent. See something completely different.'

She emitted a sound somewhere between a snort and a curious 'what?'

'I mean it. It would be good for you,' he said in a low voice. 'And good fun, too.'

Then he got up and started to fire up a barbecue grill that stood on the grass.

'Can you guess what musk oxen do if a train manages to brake in time?'

It sounded like the introduction to a joke.

'No?'

'They turn round and head-butt the locomotive.'

'It's not true!' Jane said and giggled.

'It's the truth,' Ulf confirmed without moving a muscle in his face.

He had sprayed the charcoal with lighter fluid and stood still with a match in his hand before turning to her, as if she had demanded an explanation.

'It's got to soak in for a few minutes.'

She nodded.

'Look, I bought something special because you were coming.' He rooted around in the truck and pulled out a bottle. 'It's the local aquavit. Called Musk Ox.'

She examined the hairy animal on the label. It looked like a *Star Wars* creature.

They sat down with a tumblerful each. The smell of warm lighter fluid rolled in over them in waves. Just like the shame and guilt she felt, being here with a strange man.

Ulf, too, seemed to become affected by the alcohol.

When she said 'Are they a bit like buffaloes, then?' he burst out laughing and slapped his thighs.

'Buffaloes belong to a completely different group! Musk oxen are more closely related to sheep… Think of them as giant sheep,' he advised.

She had a vision of an implausibly large, bad-tempered sheep. And they were both laughing now, though not exactly at the same thing.

Abruptly, Jane became very still. She realized that she had laughed for the first time in seven months. She stood and strode out onto the grass.

'Did I say something wrong?' Ulf asked.

She speeded up as she came closer to the charcoal grill and then focused all her strength into her right leg. Her foot struck a point low down on the lower half of the sphere. For a brief moment the whole thing floated in mid-air before the grill hit the ground. The lid shot off to the left and a cloud of ash and embers rose against the backdrop of the darkening sky.

*

Towards the end of the evening, Ulf told her about a remarkable *ethological phenomenon*. The playlist on his phone, which he had connected to two small loudspeakers placed on the window sill, was running through its loop for the fifth time and had reached the marvellous hymn from *The Lion King*. She had reached the stage of hard drinking where you feel more and more aware of yourself and hence more lost than when you started drinking. Her left elbow was forever slipping off the smooth white armrest of her plastic chair, as if one of her arms were shorter than the other. She glanced sideways at Ulf while he talked. She was ready to like him for being a traveller, a rootless person who accepted no responsibility for others, even though such descriptions were often euphemisms for *asshole*. But, in Ulf's case, everything indicated that he was a good person. There was nothing in it for him when he spent time listening to her, cooking and putting on thick workman's gloves to pick up glowing lumps of charcoal. Or when he reached out his hand to her that day in the airport.

Ulf was telling her that if one approached a herd of musk oxen closely enough for the animals to feel threatened they would form a circle around the calves.

'The calves are kept inside the circle?' Her consonants were slurred.

'That's right. The heads of the adults are all turned outwards, and their horns are lowered.'

'All pointing outwards?' She grew smaller where she sat.

'Yes, outwards. The cows decide how to form the protective circle. The mothers, in other words. And the massed horns form

49

an impenetrable wall. Nothing must harm the calves behind this barricade. Not the wolves. Nor the bears. Nothing!'

'Nothing?'

'Nothing at all.'

'SO YOU HAVE NEVER WANTED to put together a family?'
Presumably, language differences explained this kind of
thing, set phrases that simply didn't work in translation. Jane
imagined a family-making kit, a penis and a vagina screwed
together, eventually creating a complete doll's house.

'Well, no, what with writing and so on…'

Eva's eyebrows rose almost imperceptibly as she lifted the
teacup level with her self-confident, girlish breasts.

The explanation was too feeble and Jane tried again.

'I have never met the right man.'

'Of course, yes. No, I see,' Eva smiled towards Lars Christian,
who was seated in a svelte angular armchair, tapping on his
phone.

Jane clutched the edge of the seat cushion.

'But it's not too late for you,' Camilla said.

'Thanks, honey,' Jane said and winked to her.

Camilla was sitting next to her mother on the sofa. They
didn't look alike.

Camilla had her father's eyes with the flecked, blue irises of
some husky dogs and cool, symmetrical features. She practised
rhythmic gymnastics four days a week. In America, she would
have been the prettiest girl in the school.

Jane turned to look out through the window, meant to offer a view across the lake and, beyond it, Oslo's low skyline, but blocked for the duration of her stay by the yellowing side of an old trailer. The Askeland-Nilsen house had been finished only the previous month: it was a Scandinavian dream home in glass and untreated timber, and so soberly designed that one forgot just how comfortable it was, with one bathroom for each family member and iPhone-mediated temperature control. The trailer housed a young Polish couple, who so far had laid the rolls of turf, fenced the entire site, wood-stained the wall timbers and were now putting down the terrace flags. He was called Andrej or, probably, Andrzej, and, confusingly, she was Eva. Jane had taken note of bottles of vodka on a shelf above the gas cooker in the trailer. She watched the Poles from the guest room (where she slept better than she had for the last half-year) as they changed their small seating area into beds every night.

The hardest thing about staying with the Askeland-Nilsens, Jane had found, was to simulate normal breathing behaviour: she couldn't groan whenever she felt like it or keep holding her breath until she had to inhale desperately to rise to the surface. Also, she mustn't kick objects left on the stairs or howl with rage if the toothpaste didn't come out easily.

Camilla slid down from the sofa and sat instead on the rug near her father's chair.

'I can't help thinking that there are American men who feel threatened by women who... in all modesty... have got something done,' Jane said, sounding thoughtful.

Eva looked at her and sighed. For a moment, they shared

a worldwide state of female anger. Then Jane turned away to observe Lars Christian.

Her visit was quite obviously Lars Christian's doing: he was responsible for the invitation – not Eva. Jane also had a suspicion that Eva minded the intensity of that initial exchange of emails. When Lars Christian wanted to take her to the National Library in Oslo to show her the *Letters from America* collection – the bound volumes were not available for borrowing – something else suddenly came up and, taking Eva with him, he went off in the Volvo.

Jane and Lars Christian had rounded off her second evening with several glasses of red wine while watching a Norwegian variant on *Curb Your Enthusiasm* – Lars Christian did simultaneous translation and it was enjoyable. Jane was on her way to the bathroom when she noticed that the door to Camilla's bedroom was open a bit. The corridor light made a straight, narrow line that seemed to guide one's steps across the carpet all the way to the bed where it lit up Camilla's face on the pillow. Jane stopped and watched through the crack. It felt as if she was standing in the drizzle outside a huge generating station and sensed its power despite the stillness. For a long time, she stayed there with her hand on the door handle but her mind moved elsewhere in time and space. Someone came along and Jane said, unthinkingly, 'She is breathing.'

Eva stared at her, looking bewildered. Then she firmly shut the door to her daughter's room before vanishing into the bathroom without another word.

*

'Such a pity that you didn't bring any of your books,' Lars Christian said. 'They should be translated! Listen, Camilla...' and he bent over his daughter who was doing splits on a shaggy rug and touched her lightly with his foot. 'Didn't you say you'd order Jane's books on Amazon?'

Camilla looked up at him.

'Yes... I thought maybe *The Age of Plenitude*. They have it in paperback as well.'

'No need for you to worry about the price, Camilla,' Lars Christian said. 'We'll pay. Of course. Besides, it will be good to have the proper bound volumes. Then Jane can sign them. Is that all right?'

Hearing this must have made Eva consider the possibility that Jane would be staying as long as it would take to send a parcel from the USA to Europe.

'We were thinking of a trip in the car this weekend,' Lars Christian said. 'Once Martin is back home. We could visit some things worth seeing. Is that OK with you?'

'Yeah!' Camilla said.

Jane looked across to Eva, who nodded agreement. Ever since Jane had arrived, the family had been worrying away about their immediate surroundings: would she find them disappointing? But she hadn't expected to find majestic peaks rising above ice-blue fjords – it would be like believing that the Grand Canyon could be viewed from a suburb in Washington (DC).

'That sounds very nice. Even though I'm perfectly happy with this,' she said and gestured towards the caravan.

O NCE INSIDE THE DOOR of the motel room, she crashed on one of the beds and drew her knees up to her chest. And moaned.

'The whole bed is moving.'

'It's because I'm pushing at it,' Ulf told her.

'Why do you want to bring me along to go camping?' she said. Her mouth was buried in the pillow and her voice had the tone of someone about to lose a wrestling match.

'It's not camping, it's research.'

A long silence, apart from the sound of alcohol-thinned blood being pumped through her ears. She realized that her question hadn't been answered and repeated it with her eyes closed.

'Because I'm your friend in Norway,' Ulf replied.

Jane made a dissatisfied noise into the pillow.

'Because I like you. I told you so on the plane.'

He reached above her to open the window. A mild-mannered breeze blew down from the hillsides, entered past the gingham curtains and touched the crest of her hip, where the sweater had slipped up. Ulf went to the bathroom and stayed in there for a long time. She assumed that he followed some elaborate evening ritual; he had a large toilet bag for a man. Then he came back and sat down on his bed, which was separated from hers by a wooden board that cut her line of vision. To see him, she had to raise the leaden weight that was her head. His eyes were two blue fishes, each one immobile inside its individual glass bowl within a red plastic frame.

'Ulf, I'm a sixteen-year-old girl, totally inexperienced. And terrified. You won't even get to undo my bra before I start screaming.'

'So, I won't try.'

He stroked her hair. It was nice for as long as the window stayed open.

'You know, I like you, too, I think.'

'But?'

She inhaled, quickly, deeply.

'But you have no idea what it feels like to admit it.'

Dombås looked like an administrative outpost in Alaska with a tourist market thrown in. The sun beat straight down onto the sidewalk and filled the shopping street with still, amber light. Jane's state was such that she needed an effort of will to place one foot in front of the other. Ulf, on the other hand, seemed unaffected by the day before. He was wearing a slightly fitted anorak and tight, dark-blue cargo trousers. She had glimpsed his back last night: slim and shadowed by muscular ridges.

'Do you know what the Inuit call a musk ox?' he asked.

'Surely they have seven hundred different names for it?' Jane said.

She had wanted to make him laugh.

'No, they don't. A musk ox is Umingmak. The bearded one.'

'So, should I call you Umingmak?' She felt herself blush as she said that. Without planning to, her voice had gone up at least half an octave.

She followed Ulf across the parking lot. As he entered the sports shop, an electronic bell pinged. He held the door open for her. A small, silver-haired man wearing a cardigan stood behind the shop counter, so he was probably the owner. A blond woman in her twenties was unpacking clothes and placing them on a table. Jane assumed that the young woman was the owner's daughter. Ulf chatted in Norwegian with her while she measured Jane. He might be telling the assistant all kinds of things about Jane.

Finally, the assistant said in English, 'I think we had better begin with the first layer. The innermost one.'

She ushered Jane to a wall with a pegboard that displayed a collection of thick, well-designed cardboard containers, each one with its own illustration of models in underwear standing with their legs apart against a mountain backdrop. Men, women and children, like an extended family of stunningly beautiful, weatherbeaten superheroes.

Ulf's family.

'Wool or synthetic fibres?' asked the assistant.

Ulf was full of good advice at times. At other times, he seemed to be arguing with the people in the shop who presumably knew a thing or two about sports equipment but lacked his hillwalking experience. But Ulf lost interest once Jane had chosen the most expensive set of underwear in merino wool and, then, the most expensive rainwear. He hung around while she bought a sleeping bag, an inflatable pillow, a tent, freeze-dried foods, a set of pans, a knife, a hat with mosquito net and a couple of aluminium bottles.

The owner helped with choosing the right rucksack. The system of straps must be adjusted to fit her back, which was, he suggested, particularly nice and straight. It felt good to be prepared for all eventualities. It occurred to her that she had always been ill equipped. Always missing something, whatever she set out to do.

'Musk oxen? Then you must bring binoculars.'

Gosh, she should've thought of that herself.

Now and then, a price tag would lie belly-up. The cost of everything seemed perverse. She went to the changing rooms with a down-filled anorak under her arm, sat down on the stool and took two pills before confronting her face in the mirror. She suddenly remembered a red-haired mother of two in the therapy group Dr Rice had practically forced Jane to join – at the time, it was a fact that the red-haired woman had only one child, but it was usual for the members of the support groups to include the dead in their narratives, as if to make it clear that they had not been forgotten:

I had an old photo on my driving licence. I know it was old because of my eyes. I was someone else before Alison's death.

When they got to the footwear, Ulf rose from the Nike chair to let Jane sit down and went to stand by the till to chat with the owner. They glanced at her while she tried walking on the felt carpet in a pair of tall boots.

'What's the matter?' she asked.

But now Ulf was preoccupied by something the owner was pointing at outside the shop window.

She turned to the right to see herself in profile, wearing the hunting trousers and the walking boots: she could have been the first woman to cycle to Nepal in order to climb Everest without oxygen. Her mood grew still more elated as she produced her Visa card. All this gave her a quite different sensation from drifting on a river of alcohol. Pleasure was welling up from a glandular depth somewhere and wiped out the awareness of just how shallow the cause was – shopping.

The payment did not go through.

The sound of a terminated transaction brought the daughter to the counter. She stared searchingly at the card reader, as if the snag could possibly be due to it.

'Maybe there's a limit?' Ulf suggested.

'There might be,' Jane admitted.

It was much more likely that she had emptied her account. She hadn't checked the balance for months. There was a bundle of Norwegian bills in her wallet and she put the whole lot in front of the man behind the counter.

'Will this do?'

'You'll even get one of these back,' he said and handed over a crumpled green bill from the till.

It didn't matter.

O N HER FOURTH NIGHT with the Askeland-Nilsens, Eva was due at a meeting of the parents' association at Martin's school. Lars Christian was off to repair something or other in the neighbourhood along with some of the other fathers. Who would take Camilla to her training session? She offered.

At dusk, as they smoothly joined the winding coastal road, she believed all would be well. The windscreen looked out onto a rosy dream and she relaxed into a tourist's sense of alienation. Kept her eyes on the road. Kept breathing.

Camilla asked, 'Shall I put some music on?'

'I haven't got any CDs here,' Jane said.

'CDs?'

With one sweep of her index finger across the screen of her mobile, Camilla made the stereo in Jane's rented car play songs by American 'R&B queens'. Jane suppressed a question about how this could work wirelessly – she had struggled even to switch on the interior lights. She forced herself to focus on what she could see and keep her mind from picking out the trigger words in the lyrics, silly truisms about love and loss that all the same could feel like messages meant just for her.

'Turn left here.'

The girl's raised hand briefly appeared in Jane's field of vision. While Camilla looked the other way, Jane turned the volume down.

'Asker is the only town I can remember the name of,' Jane said. 'If you say it quickly, it sounds like *ask her*! And if you say it slowly, like *ass care*.'

The girl laughed and Jane took the chance to look at her. She acted the ultra-cool teen, glancing out from under heavy eyelids, blowing a strand of hair out of her face in the way of fourteen-year-old girls. But only from the neck up. Underneath the gym club's leotard, Camilla's muscles were hard as raw vegetables, proof of a willpower and discipline that Jane herself had not felt a whisper of since she was in her thirties and determined to survive as a writer. Where Camilla's long, blond hair didn't fall across her face, her skin glowed, spotless and faintly blue in the light of an oncoming car. The girl had no idea how much she mattered. Even if one told her repeatedly just how precious she was, the awareness would never truly reach someone so young. Her parents had to carry that burden.

Jane drew breath, as if she had been under water for a long time.

'Do you like it?' Camilla asked.

'Like what?'

Camilla pointed at the car stereo. Jane nodded stiffly.

'Mummy only listens to Bon Jovi.'

'Oh... I see.'

'Only when Daddy isn't at home. And she sings along. It's so-o embarrassing.'

She had a vision of Eva. The little red O in her freckled face. The glass of wine on the kitchen worktop.

'I want to lay you down, on a bed of roses...' Jane sang. She tried to put on a Norwegian accent but it came out like the Lone Ranger's Indian friend. Tonto, that was his name. Camilla laughed and snorted as she breathed in and then laughed even more at how bizarre it all sounded.

The oncoming traffic was moving slowly now. She felt that someone might suddenly open a car door or cut in ahead of them.

'Is it true that supermarkets in America keep these electric wheelchairs for customers who're too fat to walk?' Camilla asked, her mouth hanging open as if Jane had just produced this remarkable piece of information.

'Yes, it is. More or less.'

Camilla sat very still. Jane tried to imagine the girl's vision of the States.

'How long are you staying for? Are you leaving after the weekend?'

'I'm not quite sure,' Jane said.

'Mum and Dad are much nicer when you're here.'

'Really? How come?'

'I don't know. It's like, they're less stressed.'

She could see it from their point of view. The relief when a guest broke the everyday monotony. How a stranger might, for a few hours or days, change the perspective on your immediate surroundings and on who you are. But she chose to say, 'I suppose they sometimes can be a little... intense?'

Which was true, too, and anyway not necessarily a negative judgement. Eva and Lars Christian took turns to go out jogging so that one of them would always be there for the children. Lars Christian worked with people, as he put it, but was just as competent when dealing with the world of things. It was he who had taken the subtle, black-and-white photographs of running streams and fir forests that hung on the sitting room walls. She had watched as he changed the tyres on two cars within half an hour, using his own compressor and pneumatic wrench. Apparently, there were no *cable guys* in Norway. Anyway, Lars Christian had himself run fibre optic cabling into the house and set up a Wi-Fi network to which the family's many devices were connected. It was obviously just lack of time that had made him delegate tasks to the young Polish couple. Eva knitted sweaters that might have been machine-made. She had also seen Eva do cartwheels on the newly sown lawn to demonstrate a move for Camilla.

Jane had become used to people who, at best, had one talent, one gift that might be taken as God's justification for placing them on Earth. The Askeland-Nilsens excelled at all they undertook. She speculated about Martin, as yet an unknown, wondering if he would provide a natural balance. She had a vision of him: Martin would have a squint and some chronic breathing condition so they'd let him join the school football team only because it was in line with a gentle, embracing Scandinavian norm.

At the highway exit ramp, the queue of cars crawled at a snail's pace past the place where she had met the Askeland-Nilsen family on the first day. There were five cars scattered around the parking lot now, all with condensation covering the windscreens and generally in much worse shape than typical

Norwegian cars. Four pale, heavily built men stood talking in a cloud of frozen breaths next to a rusty, once-white van surrounded by empties and plastic bags. Camilla saw her looking.

'They're from Eastern Europe.'

'Do they live there?'

Camilla shrugged. 'They won't have work permits, I think. Or whatever.'

There were aspects of life in Norway that reminded Jane of stories told to her by a couple of friends who had lived in the Middle East.

On the highway, Camilla fell asleep with her head dangling between the seats. Jane gently pushed her back until she was supported against the backrest and then allowed her arm to lie for a moment across the girl's chest. She could sense the beating of Camilla's heart beneath the paper-thin material of her tracksuit. It felt as if she'd catch fire if she kept her arm there too long.

And then everything went to pieces. When they arrived at the sports hall, she was reminded of how stupid she could be at times. So dense, it was a miracle that she had managed, over and over again, to convey the opposite to her readers and the literary critics. The moment she swung the car into the parking place, it was obvious what kind of situation she had put herself in. She saw the clusters of giggling girls disappearing in through the wide glass doors. Some of them were as young as five. She clutched the steering wheel and could feel her pulse beating under her nails.

The tablets were in her suitcase. In the guest room.

'I'll wait here,' she said.

Camilla said, with her head tilted sideways, 'You can't wait here. I'll be training for two and a half hours.'

'No problem at all.' She sounded as snappy as if at a public reading and the organizer had forgotten to provide water.

'No, please. Come in and watch – you must. You'll get icy cold in the car.'

'I'll be fine, just fine. I can listen to your music.'

Jane looked at the recess on the dashboard. Camilla's mobile was no longer there.

Camilla took the phone from her pocket and handed it over.

'It actually has the songs for my training programme but I guess that's all right. Usually, they're on the CD player as well...' She stopped and then went on. 'Don't you *want* to watch me?'

Jane swallowed several times before she met Camilla's eyes. Smiling seemed to rip her face apart.

'Yes, of course I do.'

B Y EARLY SPRING OF 1996, the year Jane met Greg, more than thirty churches with predominantly black congregations had caught fire in the Southern states. In February, the *Washington Post* reported that the majority of these incidents had indisputably been cases of arson. NationsBank, the savings bank based in the South, had offered half a million dollars to anyone providing information that led to the arrest and sentencing of the perpetrators. In June, President Clinton called for action: *We must all do our part to end this rash of violence* and went on to say *I have vivid and painful memories of black churches being burnt in my own state when I was a child* (later, doubts were raised that there had in fact been any outbreaks of racially motivated church arson in Arkansas during Clinton's childhood).

New York University, where Jane was enrolled as a student of literature, was far from Tennessee and Alabama, but a combination of opportunity and an attack of bad conscience meant that she was swept along in a peaceful march of anti-racist demonstrators on their way to the United Nations building. She and her friend Alice had been to a Gustav Klimt exhibition at the Frick. On the walk back to her rooms in Broome Street, she found herself going against the flow of the march and felt like a distressed fish swimming against the shoal. For a while,

67

she zigzagged along the sidewalk, pressed herself against the walls of buildings and stood for quite a long time behind a fire hydrant with a growing sense of being somehow in the wrong, just because she wanted something different from everyone else. That very morning, she and Alice had had a philosophical discussion over breakfast – a familiar mix of Sunday morning gloom and youthful self-absorption – and had agreed that they were both creatures of the Western world, self-centred and privileged people who never helped anyone but themselves, and hardly even that.

Finally, Jane gave up. It was pointless saying things like 'I'm sorry' or 'I've gone the wrong way'. Instead, faced with the crowd of humanity, she joined them and muttered the slogan to herself but in unison with the others: *No Justice, No Peace*.

When the march passed Grand Central Station, her eye was caught by a tall young man who was walking just a few steps ahead of her and spoke the words with passion. His hair was halfway to his shoulders and he looked like Abraham Lincoln, if it was possible to imagine the sixteenth president as a twenty-something student who had never carried the responsibility for a nation at war, and dressed like Kurt Cobain. She had seen that guy before but couldn't think where. Pondering this, she took care not to lose sight of him. Eventually, they came to march side by side and, in the surrounding chaos that made looking every which way quite reasonable, their eyes often met. On East 45th Street, the young man turned to Jane and shouted a question into her ear. Did she know where they were going?

'Don't you know?' she shouted back.

'No, I just came along for the ride. I was on my way home.'

'You're kidding?'

'I had no idea about the demonstration.'

She shook her head.

'But now I'm here, which is a good thing.'

'We're glad you feel the same way,' she said.

It took a few weeks before Jane admitted that they had been in the same situation. Meanwhile, they had slept with each other twice and he had bought her a ring from a vending machine, knelt in front of her in the line to a Stone Temple Pilots gig, and asked her to be his lover. It turned out that they were not only at the same university but actually in the same department. Greg had joined the creative writing course and definitely had ambitions to become a writer. Jane was in her second year of the course in English literature and shared his ambition but kept it secret. The similarities between them didn't end there. They came from the same state, though Greg had grown up in La Crosse. Both used to watch *Scooby-Doo* after school and, just like Jane, Greg stayed with the programmes that followed it, *Gilligan's Island* and *The Love Boat*, despite the mental pain they caused. Separately, they had both flirted with vegetarianism but only in short bursts because they read the same anxiety-making article in *New Scientist* about the crucial role of amino acids in brain development (they had both come across the magazine in a dentist's waiting room). As for beers, Greg preferred Pabst Blue Ribbon, a drink to which Jane's father had devoted his life, more or less. They discovered that Jane, on her first independent holiday, had stayed at a campsite not at all far from Greg's childhood home and had actually bought painkillers in a pharmacy run by Greg's uncle. Before his stroke, that was.

And it came back to her where she had seen Greg before. Not in the university – their timetables scarcely overlapped at all – but at a reading in the KGB Bar. It had been hard for her to take her eyes off him on that occasion, too. Later, they read in the *Militant* (Greg, who was obviously a socialist at the time, subscribed to it) that some 1,200 people had marched in the demo against the church arsonists. *And the two individuals who were meant for each other happened to join the procession at exactly the same place!* Neither Jane nor Greg was especially religious or superstitious, but they were both at the age when you can't help letting yourself suspect that there is a plan for the universe and that your name is at least mentioned in it.

Jane knew already after their first night together in her place on Broome Street that she wanted to marry him. She wanted a quick, unannounced ceremony in some place with no connections to either of them. Partly because she found that scenario much more romantic than dressing up like a cupcake and proceeding to do exactly what billions of couples had done before. But her main reason was to escape her parents who would, without fail, envelop the whole event in the usual murk of pointless grief and disapproval. She saw all this clearly after having woken up before him, rolled over on her side and, supporting herself on her elbow, looking at him in the dust-laden light. She examined his face with its faint grey shadow around the mouth and chin but deep in childish sleep. A long, slender arm stuck out from under the blanket. His fingers twitched. They had none of the repulsiveness of other men's fingers.

He woke when she was on her way to the bathroom.

'You're not going anywhere, are you?'

She sank down on the bed next to him.

'I should be off to a Sigma Theta Lambda meeting.'

'What for?'

'What for? I've said I'll be there, silly. That's why.'

They both smoked. In bed. Looking back on it ten years later, it seemed like a ritual from a lost past, as distant as duels with pistols or mummification.

'But you don't actually want to join a student soc talking shop.'

'How do you know?'

'You dislike all that stuff. Basically, you don't want to be a member of anything.'

'Don't I?'

'No. You'd like to get out of it. But it worries you to think that not joining in will make you into a sad, lonely person.'

'The things you know.'

'But all true?'

Jane was twenty-two years old. She was still not sure what kind of person she was. 'But, well...'

'Now you don't need to worry about being sad and lonely any more,' Greg said and caressed her cheek.

And so, with an untroubled conscience, she did what she truly wanted to do, which was to be on her own or with Greg, busy writing, studying, drifting around New York or being indoors looking out over the big city, or going out for drinks to merge into the crowd, maybe two to three times a month.

Greg was not particularly involved in student life either, even though he was far more of an extrovert than Jane. He was one of those rare people who is just as much at ease chatting with gang members as passing the time of day with an old lady and making her chortle. He played in a band.

Until she met Greg, Jane had been lonely. Lonely as an only child, lonely hanging out with Alice and other girls, lonely going out with boys who made out they were listening while all their attention was in their pawing hands. College had saved her from the dreariness of the Midwest, and literature from the sensation of being somehow locked into her own head. In Greg she had found the first person with whom she could connect strongly. It felt like having searched radio frequencies all alone for twenty-two years before finding a voice at last.

With him, she did things she had never done with her old boyfriends back in Wisconsin.

'Oh-la-la...' Alice said when Jane told her this.

Jane had to explain.

'Not that kind of thing. Or, yes. That, too. But what I really meant was things like sitting on a moth-eaten sofa listening while he practises with his band. When he went back to La Crosse for his uncle's funeral, I had to keep sniffing at a T-shirt he had left behind.'

After a month with Greg, she met his parents. He had told her in advance that they were much like her own mother and father: tedious, cold, loveless. The weekend in New York with Peggy and John Noland made Jane wonder what other features of their life together Greg had hyped up for her. Not that it really mattered; she took his wanting to be more like her as an incomprehensible but tremendous compliment.

John, Greg's father, was a jovial, bearded man who wrote books on local history. He spent weekends and holidays re-enacting Civil War battles in the company of other jovial, bearded men. He had rigged up a real cannon on his driveway and fired it once a year where it stood, regardless of any local police permission. He was also a pacifist. He had fought in Vietnam and learnt a thing or two about people, as he said. Peggy had been Miss Teen Colorado and later kicked up a lot of controversy by stating in public that beauty competitions were not only bad news for women in general but also gave the master of ceremonies opportunities to fiddle with underage girls. The only conceivably *tedious* side of Peggy and John Noland was that they owned and ran a company trading in spare parts for agricultural machinery. As for *loveless*, this seemed to apply exclusively in the physical sense. At a lunch in Central Park, they spoke openly about their plan to divorce when Greg had started school. This had been postponed because of the children and, having reached the last milestone when Greg's little brother Jeff moved out of the parental home, they had become so accustomed to their platonic marriage that they could not imagine another kind of relationship.

'Anyway, we are working together,' Peggy explained.

'Sex, now, we've forgotten what it's about,' John added. He glanced at Greg. 'I hope there's no more you'll need to ask on the subject, son.'

'We sure couldn't help you with that kind of thing,' Peggy said.

Then they laughed so loudly people at the tables around them turned and stared.

This was who they were, Peggy and John Noland. They had a lot to do with Greg being who he was. More than before, Jane dreaded him meeting her parents; their eccentricities were

73

the opposite of fun. Also, they were older than his parents: she had been their longed-for child, a late blessing, even though it rarely felt like that.

As she said to Greg after the weekend with his parents, 'You know I told you how I think of my childhood? As a cryptic place populated by people you can't help feeling are strangers? And you nodded.'

'Yes.'

'Yes?'

'I nodded because I thought that was beautifully put,' Greg said.

Jane found that describing her parents' oddities to Greg was a surprisingly positive experience. This was not only because he often laughed but also because she came across as an almost more interesting person against the grim background, just as the story of any passionate emotion can add a new dimension to one's opinion of somebody. But her stories had been given a wry, anecdotal quality and been subject to her own edits; for Greg to meet her parents in real life would be quite different. What would he think when her father came out with one of his conspiratorial monologues about America as the lost paradise? Probably that it helped to explain her prevailing pessimism. And when her mother tried to cover up another attack of depression by dishing up a non-stop series of labour-intensive meals and snacks – would Greg fear that her agitated version of melancholia was heritable? Would he realize why their house did not feel like a home but a small, rock-panelled shrine that served as a place of refuge from life?

After their decision to spend Christmas with her parents – just how they came to agree on it was permanently clouded by the enigmatic fog of love – her worries grew more precise. What would Greg make of the tradition of having three Christmas trees (one natural and green, one coated in silver and another in blinding white), spray-painted by her father in the garage, decorated by her mother in a manic pre-Christmas frenzy but seen only by very few others because her parents hardly ever had guests?

'Jane, listen,' he said while they waited for Robert to pick them up outside the arrivals hall at Mitchell Airport. 'For all I care, your parents could have lobster claws and glow in the dark. It's you I want.'

The full range of Greg's social skills was revealed to her during that Christmas holiday. If she had not been in love with him, she might just have found his behaviour rather too chameleon-like. Had she not married him and spent eighteen years at his side, Jane might even have remembered him as manipulative.

Consider, for example, his reaction to *the quiet hours*.

'The quiet hours?' Greg's face had the expression of someone ready to be told of a new party game.

All four of them were in the living room on the first night of the visit. Jane considered grabbing the marble ashtray on the coffee table and beating herself senseless with it.

'Jane can explain what it is,' Robert said. 'She has grown up with our quiet hours.'

'Oh, Dad,' she hissed.

'Jane,' Dorothy whispered, perched on the edge of her armchair.

The small decorative cushions crowded Jane where she sat next to Greg on the two-seater sofa. The spotless, moss-green carpet was a quagmire about to swallow her tennis sock-clad feet.

Dorothy's eyes somehow showed that her jaw muscles had tightened beneath her plump cheeks.

Robert turned to Greg. 'It's simple. We have agreed to be completely at rest between five and seven in the afternoon.'

Jane had an urge to add that this was in consideration of her mother's state of mind, and that the quiet hours had actually been advised by a psychotherapist, but realized that the information would hardly help to normalize the family ritual.

Greg looked from one to the other, then raised his index finger and said, 'I truly get this. People don't take the time off just to *be* any more. Everyone seems to have forgotten the importance of… contemplation. How much space do we give it nowadays?'

She saw her father look appraisingly at Greg and allocate him to the category 'self-important college kid'. She noticed how Greg's slightly hooked, lovable Lincoln-nose seemed larger seen sideways on and wanted to pull him back in the sofa and out of the danger zone. But he avoided looking at her and, with a big smile on his face, addressed Dorothy.

'And besides it's good to chill now and then.'

Unbelievably, this made her parents burst out laughing.

Greg glanced at the clock.

'But there are still six more minutes to go before the quiet hours begin,' he said. 'Now, how shall we pass the time?'

He was *teasing* them. He was the first person in history *to tease anyone* inside the Ashland family house. But it seemed to work all right.

'Jane tells me you play in a rock band,' Robert said.

Dorothy rose to tidy away their juice glasses and the crumb-filled platter that had held their hot tuna sandwiches.

Greg replied, 'I play lead guitar.' And went on explaining, as if it would interest her father in the slightest – her dad, whose music recordings amounted to two Kris Kristofferson cassettes for respectively the car and the workshop: 'Strictly speaking, I shouldn't call it *lead* because I'm the band's only guitarist.'

The rectangular shadow of the mailman's van rumbled past on the snowy road at the end of their drive. It reached the stop sign and its brake lights cast a red glow in between the curtains.

'Are you Jewish, Gregory?'

'Not that I know of. Now and then people ask me, though.'

'Jane tells us that you're a socialist,' her father continued.

'Guilty as charged,' Greg said loudly and put his hand up.

Dorothy's tidying took on the darting speed of a reptile. Jane clutched Greg's hand and glanced at her father only to find that his face didn't look as she had expected. His bluish jowls shuddered like a basset hound's and his eyes were rimmed with moist resignation.

'To the best of my knowledge, I've never met a socialist before.'

The next day, Greg was entrusted with spray-painting the silver tree. Jane stood in the garage doorway and watched. Robert held the tree at arm's length; Greg wore a face mask and carried out his painting task with easy, almost dancing movements.

'Suppose you've had experience with all the graffiti,' Robert said.

Greg even managed to encourage her mother into uttering more than two or three sentences at a time. He praised the stuffing for the goose and paid attention when she told him about the classic recipe by James Beard and the critical balance to be struck between prunes and Madeira.

'She can be quite interesting, don't you think?' was how Greg put it when they were alone in Jane's room. 'She has an artistic soul.'

'But no artistic talent.'

'Could be.'

They didn't make love in Jane's old room but she felt as if they had; as if she had returned inside a different body, desecrated her childhood home and then rejected it (like an ex-prisoner spending the night, just as a joke, in the old, now abandoned prison – this was the best metaphor the aspiring writer could come up with). Just being there with Greg and thinking *never again*; never again the absolute stillness of the Sunday mornings, never again her mother's half-hour of pretend-reading the same double-page spread in the *Milwaukee Journal*. Never again the feeling that love was a limited commodity that had to be rationed.

At night, she lay with Greg and held him tightly until she sensed her grip on him slip as sleep came. Then she dreamt that Greg was not there and that she was Jane alone, in Jane's bed. And Jane was not a student of literature with her own home address on Broome Street, New York City – only Jane. Alone.

The whole spring semester had felt like only a few days. They were young, in love, full of hope and living in the place better suited to such people than anywhere else in the world (eight years later, they made a honeymoon trip to Paris, a city they agreed afterwards to be a great deal sadder and shabbier than New York). They wrote. They read. They hung out with Greg's friends in the band and frequented small, smoke-filled music bars. Until the band dropped him.

Jane had never played an instrument but it became obvious even to her that Greg was not a great guitarist. Listening to the others speaking about him, especially towards the end, opened her eyes. She suspected that he had been asked to join them because of his alternative-style persona, the way he dressed, wore his hair and, not least, his easy charm. But, seemingly, he lacked the crucial thing.

'Am I a bit out?'

'Dude, listen, you've been waltzing right through. Wrong beat.'

'Oops, it wasn't syncopated then?'

'Yeah… the last tune was.'

It was almost impossible to understand, especially when you saw Greg move. She could lie in the bed alcove in the small apartment, full of delight as she watched him making coffee: his hands had such perfect awareness of space and distance that he handled everything without fumbling. He seemed at ease in the present. Was that not also a kind of musicality?

Whatever, they did not want him in The Hard Stains.

Jane did her best to create a version of events that could be lived with.

'Of course, they totally lack direction.'

'Do you think so?' Greg said.

'Sure, all their new songs are stuffed with over-technical rhythmic notations.'

'Yeah?'

'I mean, there was a clear trend towards progressive metal.' She said this with her upper lip curled to indicate a musical expertise. Meanwhile, she suppressed the thought it had only been a few months since she had said goodbye at last not only to stone-washed jeans with high waistbands but to all her glam metal rock mixtapes.

They had even more time to be together. Her belongings increasingly ended up in his Brooklyn place, which was a few square metres larger than hers and less full of oppressive student clutter. There they would sit, each on a kitchen chair, looking past the edge of the window-mounted air conditioning unit to catch glimpses of New Jersey. They smoked too much and talked until the early morning, about lecturers and their quirks, about form and content in the novel. They would speculate about news stories like the one about the elderly Palestinian teacher who had, in February, shot wildly in all directions from the top of the Empire State Building and murdered – out of all the innocent people on the observation deck – a promising Danish musician, whom Greg had met several times. Another musician, a band member and friend of the dead man, was shot in the head but survived. Like Mayor Giuliani, Jane and Greg joined the many-hundred-strong crowd that went to the Bellevue Hospital where a separate room had been set aside for the visitors.

The story of the gunman on the observation deck was one of many events that spring which contributed to Jane and Greg's suspicion – typical of their age and time – that *the world was fucking with them.* The feeling of injustice stayed with Jane, for how was one to live in a world that seemed especially intent on killing off young and good people?

There was just an ounce of truth in this immature intimation of martyrdom. Young adults are easy prey. Greg and Jane noticed it as soon as they sneaked outside: he in his second-hand clothes, she still shy about her femininity, and both so polite and diffident, with outrage just below the skin and cash from casual jobs in their pockets. Their unease at not being taken seriously would radiate from them with blushing, shining rays that attracted all the assholes they ever met:

'You look like you could do with our bargain offer on a year's supply of essential vitamins and minerals.' Or:

'Correct, there is legislation establishing tenants' rights in New York, but in this case the rent can be raised with immediate effect because…' Or:

'Do you have to sit at this table? This gang here is a whole law firm that…'

All of which added to Jane's conviction that the two of them were up against an entire world full of warmongers, financed by advertising.

They made love and made love again, and planted chilli and pepper seeds in pots lined up on the window sill in an attempt to save money, but their optimism faded as they observed the sad-looking, black soil; they listened to post-hardcore rock tapes featuring Shelter or Fugazi and became militant vegans (though they were not quite sure what the 'militant' bit entailed).

And he stared at her body and wanted to have her all the time but not in that way, it wasn't like that, because she could see straight through to his innermost self, and it no longer bothered her that he was not a guitarist in a band, he could be what he liked and it wouldn't change anything. Unless he was a brewery salesman or a trader in agricultural spare parts.

Christ, no. Never, never become the living dead, like Robert and Dorothy.

Like Robert and Dorothy? You've got to be kidding. They love each other, for a start. But check out my parents! My mom and dad – what can I say? Just think about it. Divorced in spirit ages ago. Sticking together mostly to have each other to pick at. Like an ever-lasting negotiation. Spaces they define as his or hers, just to get away from each other.

So? What about my dad's workshop? Have you thought about that?

A shed workshop, that's nothing. My dad is like an impotent museum curator. He has the largest collection of Union Army-issue water canteens in the world.

I know, but it's so much better to own loads of water canteens than to have no reason for living at all, like my mom.

True. But I love you and we'll never become like them.

No, we'll never be like that.

Never.

Jane and Greg had their first serious row outside John Updike's childhood home in Shillington, Pennsylvania. They had been together for a year and now it was summer again. Shillington was the first stop in their Great Literary Odyssey – that is, a four-day car holiday. The trip had acquired its splendid title during a night of scribbling down possible places to visit on the back of a beer mat. They would go from New York to Shillington, and then head south, to Richmond, where Edgar Allan Poe spent his childhood years. Next, they would cross the border into North Carolina and try to find O. Henry's birthplace in Greensboro before ending their long journey in what they felt was the Mecca for devotees of the art of fiction: Savannah, Georgia, where Flannery O'Connor had bred peafowl and written her stories.

This itinerary that, without time for breaks, added up to more than twenty-four hours of driving, proved something about their youthful chutzpah and lack of common sense as well as – and this was the conclusion Jane and Greg preferred when they recalled that summer holiday – that they loved each other very much. They had borrowed a Civic without air conditioning and bought a carton of Marlboros. She was going to wear knee-length skirts in flowery materials and cowboy boots, like the young, rootless women in the films about violence and romance that were much admired at the time. He was to take black-and-white pictures of her. Both would enter inspired fragments of writing in the leather-bound notebook each had brought. Clearly, a plan with scope for disappointments.

A storm front was chasing them during their first day on the road. At dusk, when they reached Shillington, a bruise-blue cloud bank rolled over the car roof towards the horizon where it spread out and, by then fit to burst, erupted in flashes of lightning. Shillington was not a town on its own, as they had thought, but a development on the edge of Reading, which wasn't much of a town in the first place. The wind grew stronger as they drove endlessly along the ruler-straight roads lined with neat, two-storey brick houses and kept a lookout for Philadelphia Avenue. John Updike presented a problem, anyway: he was alive. Jane found this especially troubling. Because the other three writers on their itinerary were long since dead and buried, tracing them was a romantic pilgrimage, an appealing as well as appropriate task for young people with an interest in literature. On the other hand, rubbernecking outside the childhood home of a great living author was somehow quite different. It felt like hero-worship or the kind of thing crazy people did.

The wind blew over the roofs of the buildings and through the heavy summer canopies of the trees. Wet, green leaves rained down on the car and briefly jammed the wipers before fluttering nervously and disappearing across the windscreen. No one was to be seen on the trim lawns. It wasn't the weather for enjoying the hammocks on the porches, where they were swinging senselessly on thin chains. There was no access to mobile phones or GPS navigation; it would be another year before Google became a registered trademark. Their map was a poor copy taken from a road atlas in the New York Public Library, and when they saw a street name that meant they had driven even farther away from the avenue where Updike had once lived, they homed in, like insects, on the dome of light over the football stadium. They tried three times to find someone in the stadium parking lot to ask the way, but despite all the parked cars it was as deserted as everywhere else, so they gave up and found a Best Western hotel in Reading.

The room had a double bed that vibrated if you fed a quarter in a slot and was covered with a pale brown, knobbly bedspread.

The seed of their disagreement was sown in this room. The background was that, a week earlier, Greg had asked Jane to read a short story he had written. Critiquing his work was one of her least favourite things. She had told herself during the past year that her sense of unease about Greg's writing was due to her being so close to the writer that their very closeness prevented her from relating to the text in an appropriate way. It was an excellent explanation, as such: it was complex, made sense psychologically, was nicely linked to their relationship and shared high-flown ideas about the complexity of reading and writing. It was even in line with the dominant literary theory at the time, which insisted that proper reading must be done without reference to the lived life of the author. The only problem was that the explanation did not fit the case.

'Jane, have you read that short story yet?'

'Ye-es,' she said hesitatingly.

She made for the bathroom and locked the door behind her, but heard his voice through the plasterboard walls.

'What do you think? Why haven't you said anything?'

The double question meant that she could delay a little longer.

'I guess I was waiting for you to ask.'

To see your own mirror image, not the face of the man you were talking to.

'Well?' Greg said.

She turned her lower lip inside out, moved her lower jaw from side to side.

'Well... what?' she said in the end.

'What do you think?'

85

Both toothbrushes stood in a plastic glass on the shelf above the sink. She pushed her toothbrush closer to his so that the bristles touched. She had waited for too long to reply.

'I think it was good.'

She dreaded leaving the bathroom. If she had to tell him the truth, he was sure to react as he had when he was asked to give up playing in the band – with exaggerated reasonableness.

(Without his knowledge The Hard Stains had been booked to do a demo tour with a professional skateboard team. They would play in twelve cities during the summer and actually be paid to play while the skaters performed for the audience. The contract had been negotiated without Greg as a partner in the deal.)

Bursts of rain hammered on a small window above the toilet. She somehow heard him waiting for her answer, imagined him lying on the bed with his hands under his head and looking up at the motionless fan in the ceiling. She had a vision of herself emerging naked from the bathroom, going over to sit on him and make him forget about asking questions.

The truth was this: Greg was incisive, clear-headed and intuitive but when he put pen to paper, he wrote like a man who has lost control. She had almost come to think of it as a failure of coordination, a brain-hand issue, like that affecting Drew back in the elementary school who simply couldn't place his right hand on his heart and recite the first words in the Pledge of Allegiance at the same time. However many years he practised, it made no difference. In moments of honesty with herself, Jane had to admit that Greg seemed to create a literary world of shadows where there was little genuine thought and too many knowing literary devices. His work might give an impression of profundity at first but, on closer reading, the text was only obscure. A leading character might be thinking something, using too many words, while walking city streets or possibly looking out through a window. There seemed to be little else. Apart, that is, from a dream of being a writer. In his latest short story – the one he wanted her to talk about now – one thing *had* left a serious impression on her. It was a major mistake made on the first page where a casual reference to a dog had surely slipped into the description of the male protagonist. At least, the text read: *He lit another cigarette. Then he crossed the pedestrian area on his hind legs.*

Jane felt it should be possible to charm her way out of all this. She showered, for what could be more natural after a long journey in a car? She joined Greg on the bed afterwards and said something about great forward movement in his narrative, a very special atmosphere. That kind of thing.

'That kind of thing?'

'Yes.'

The next morning, standing outside Updike's childhood home, he kept prodding her. The row that followed contained pointers to how their respective roles would play out whenever they disagreed: she got angry even though it was he who had reason to be, while he grew talkative even though she was better at using words. When he felt hurt, he expressed it. When she felt hurt, she started a counter-attack.

Afterwards, Jane couldn't remember much of what had been said, other than her telling Greg the truth about his writing – but in a raised voice, as if she had been offended against. Much clearer in her mind was the impression left by Updike's house, which had become a doctor's surgery. It had a name plate on the wall and the open area in front was littered with broken branches and rubbish, blown there like driftwood. A narrow, flagstone path led to the doctor's waiting room. Because patients were lumbering past now and then, they had to light new cigarettes and try not to sound as if they were dealing with a crisis. During these interruptions, standing in that mercilessly exposed place, they learnt what it feels like to fight with the person you love when you have no experience of what it is like to fight with the person you love. It means that the method of arguing, the phrases, the very facial expressions are taken straight out of film and novels, or out of possible memories of arguments between your parents. The desperation stays in your mind, and the taste in your mouth of all the cigarettes that were dragged on and then dropped in the grass and flattened under the smooth sole of a stupid cowboy boot. You still don't know from experience that rows usually end by your swift return to the all-forgiving present, with your self-regard still largely intact. And you still believe in the serious intent of every word said, and dread losing the person you love because it will kill you, and you sink into solemn grief because you have not yet been ground down by life into a less self-important version of yourself.

Despite the lasting bad feeling between them, they completed one more stage in the planned journey: the Edgar Allan Poe museum, which was very appropriately unnerving. Greg did not seem bitter but the dancing lightness in him was gone. He must have been so deeply shaken that Jane could hardly bear her own bad conscience. They dragged themselves from room to room, looking at Poe's handwritten manuscripts, which neither of them had the energy to try to decipher. The shrill voice of the guide. The feeling of being awkwardly young and prone to nervous yawning and febrile sweating and unable to follow anything that was said.

This silver-plated coffee jug belonged to Poe's sister's foster family. This pair of Old Sheffield candlesticks belonged to a woman to whom Poe dedicated a poem.

This shabby, narrow Gothic chair tells you nothing because your heart beats far too fast and, besides, you have developed a strange heat eczema that is crawling down your neck and breasts and will make him hate you even more.

Cigarettes and more cigarettes, and afterwards, in the parking lot, you see no fewer than four young women wearing the same skirt as you. And his hand is limp, it doesn't squeeze yours hard in return.

So they returned home, Jane to Broome Street and Greg to Brooklyn, and she heard nothing more from him.

She left long messages on his answering machine, using more stock phrases from films and TV series. She told him things she hadn't said to anyone before and would never say again. There is an age for telling someone that *I'm nothing without you* and sounding truthful, perhaps because it is true. Then, it is possible to believe that you are who you are only because the person you love has loved you.

She called Peggy Noland, who told her that Greg was not at home with them in La Crosse.

'I thought you two would've got to somewhere in Tennessee by now?'

She went round to his place and listened at the door. She waited in the stairs until four in the morning but he didn't come. The summer heat in New York and the grief over her love turned into one and the same thing. Sleep was impossible, thought was impossible.

After a week, he stood outside her door. He was wearing a red-checked shirt with cut-off sleeves and a baseball cap with a Marshall logo. She feared that all he wanted was to pick his things up, that they would never meet again. At the same time, she was relieved that the torment of waiting would be over. Recently, she'd worried that it might bring on a ruptured blood vessel in the brain and speculated about how many days in a row you can tolerate a high pulse rate before the damage is done.

She let him in and stood with her back against the kitchen alcove, waiting for him to tell her if it was all over or not by the place he chose to sit down. Would he sit on her bed? Or at the low, crescent-shaped kitchen table he could barely fit his knees under? That was the place a visitor would choose. But he remained standing in the middle of the room. A week earlier, it had been her undisputed right to stick her spoon into his ice cream or snatch a can of Coke from his hand and drink from it. She could have gone to him and put her hand on his crotch. As exceptional and unaccustomed as that contract between them had felt at first, as extraordinary was its possible cancellation just now.

'Jane, I've done some thinking. Actually, quite a lot,' Greg said.

She looked fixedly at her feet on the linoleum flooring.

'I no longer believe that I will be a writer,' he continued.

Her relief that he had perhaps not come to end it all made her shoulders less tense. She had to focus not to sound thrilled by what he had just told her.

'Greg, listen,' she said. 'That's not the point.'

How hollow it sounded. But whatever he became made not the slightest difference. She cared for only one thing: would they still be together?

Even so, she had to carry on.

'It's not the same as becoming a plumber or a dentist. It's not about a straight choice. It's about taking a step at a time.'

He took his cap off and slapped it against his thigh as if he had been out on a dusty country road.

'You must work out if writing is for you. If you enjoy it. Not if you want to *be a writer*.'

'Sure. So, I've decided I won't write.'

Cautiously, she walked up to him, stopped at arm's length and, standing on tiptoe, pulled her fingers through his hair. It was sticky where the cap had been.

'I'm sweating. It's a killer heat out there.'

'But why are you thinking like this?'

'Your voice tells me you know why,' he replied, but didn't sound as if he blamed her.

She was about to start crying and had to look away. 'Because of what I said?'

'Because you were right in what you said. My course teachers have told me roughly the same. So have some people in the class. But you're the only one among them who can't possibly have an ulterior motive.'

'Greg, come here.' She led him to the bed and they sat down together.

'Whatever happens, we will need one decent income,' he went on. 'One of us should go for a steady job. Stands to reason who it should be.'

His hands were still on the bedspread. He was looking into the future.

'But, I'd like to be... well, connected to literature. I mean, professionally, somehow. Oh, I don't know.'

'Like, say, a librarian?'

'Maybe.'

He took her hand.

'Jane, you mustn't cry.'

'I'm not crying. I love you.'

'I know.'

'Are you sure it isn't worth trying to write a little more?' She turned away from him to dry her tears. He pulled out a cigarette from his breast pocket with his free hand and left it dangling between his lips. She reached out for matches and lit it for him.

'There are two kinds of people in this world...' Greg began.

'Those who say there're two kinds of people in the world, and those who don't?' Jane suggested.

'Listen.' He inhaled, then exhaled and the smoke swirled lazily across the floor. 'There are those who deliver and those who receive. I mean it. Consider yourself. You read a third of what I read. You hardly ever talk about books. You're critical of practically all forms of culture, TV programmes, films, whatever. Even baseball games. I think you don't experience such things the same way I do. You don't get taken in. You sit there, thinking of how differently you'd have gone about it. If you had cared to try in the first place, that is. Constant analysis. For example, think about our trip.'

'The thought of losing you had left me nearly comatose.'

'I know, but before that. Not finding Updike's house wouldn't have bothered you at all. I know you think that any damn thing can be turned into narrative. So, you had no need to see that house, or any other. For inspiration, or anything like that. I'm sure you had gathered enough material for three short stories before we crossed the Pennsylvanian border.'

So, he had understood how the creative part of her mind worked.

'But, I… I'm not like you,' he said. 'I'm almost the opposite. And I'm fine with that for as long as I can see that you succeed.'

So dearly did he love her.

Jane dedicated her first book to Greg. The launch date was 16th March 2000. It was impossible to forget the date. Three years later, on that same day, their daughter Julie was born.

S HE WALKED UP the brick steps to the sports hall with the seizure lingering in her body like a muscular hum. She smiled at the woman who came down the steps with a couple of hula hoops in her hand and used her coat sleeve to wipe off a dribble of spit. It had begun after the usual signs: the smell of sun-warmed gravel, and hair that should have been washed, the sight of autumn leaves in a sandbox.

Once inside, she followed the sounds of the authoritative voices of coaches shouting above the beat of Eurodisco. She opened a door to a huge gym with a hangar-like, domed roof that made her head swim once more. Stepping over boots, water bottles and Hello Kitty bags, she went to sit on a low wooden bench along a wall covered with wooden bars. Camilla was on the exercise mat, dancing and doing cartwheels with a candy-coloured ball. Her face was red, as if she had been crying. Then the beat of the music changed and, at the same time, there was a piercingly nasal call from a female coach. Camilla went up on her toes holding the ball in her hands before sinking to her knees and arching the upper part for her body backwards in a move with echoes of adult sensuality. She stayed in position, her bottom against her heels, rolling the ball across her chest between the palms of her hands.

Jane nodded to the mothers sitting next to her on the bench. Every one of them wore tall rubber boots laced at the top. Their faces had obviously been attended to with much care. She was glad to have escaped twitching with cramps on the floor in front of this lot, in front of anyone. That hadn't happened since the day she dropped in to deliver her car to Tom. Her place of choice was a toilet, preferably one for the disabled – she could deal with the bouts of shivering on her own by seeing the joins between the tiles as vanishing lines in a perspective. Afterwards she would feel stiff and sore, as if she had been walking for too long in ill-fitting shoes. The intense sense of awareness that each one of us stands alone on this Earth usually persisted for a couple of hours.

There were at least forty girls on the floor, all of them beautiful. Their concentration made them turn all their attention inwards, into an inner hall of mirrors, shiny and glittering, with a flawless floor. And then she made a discovery: some of these girls danced and turned with the bloodless precision of small steel devices covered in stretch Lycra. It made her shiver again, like an aftershock of the shaking that had sent her into the toilet.

Three of the coaches were from Eastern Europe. Jane wasn't sure that she could hear the difference between native Norwegian and, say, Polish Norwegian, but she observed their Slavic features and their hard make-up, which fleetingly made her think: 'prostitutes'. The older lady who was supervising Camilla looked like a native, though. She had parked herself at the edge of the mat, next to the chair with the CD player, and was shouting. Every time Camilla let the ball slip and stood still, hesitating while the music continued, her coach emitted a loud snorting noise from deep inside her sinuses. The girl smiled apologetically and carried on. Jane watched as the young body grew steadily more self-conscious, its movements more forced. She sensed rather than saw a faint shoulder tremor. At one point, the coach ran up to the girl and slapped her thigh. Jane just stopped herself from crying out.

When the ball rolled away after yet another uncoordinated pirouette, Camilla buried her face in her hands.

Jane got up. She was only too aware of how out of place she would look out there on the exercise mats: shapely, adult, wearing a coat, as she stepped into the flow of raucous music. The coach had already reached Camilla, taken hold of her upper arm with a two-fingered pincer grip, as if touching an insect, and pulled her up. Camilla turned her face away. Unheeding, the other girls carried on with their moves. The mothers on the bench glanced briefly at the scene, then located their own daughters in the crowd and smiled.

As Jane started out towards the middle of the floor, the coach came closer to Camilla, picked up the ball and squeezed it under her arm. Jane heard her whisper something at the same time as she moved her right hand from the girl's arm to her waist and pinched a small fold of skin and leotard between thumb and index finger while shaking her head. Jane was pretty sure she had seen all she needed. Camilla twisted herself free and ran past Jane.

'Camilla, wait!'

Jane had a good idea of what the coach had said to Camilla, something about being overweight, which was absurd not only because the girl was so thin, but was quite out of order in any

97

case. As she got closer to the coach, it became obvious that she kept nodding uncontrollably: tiny, twitchy head movements that made her grey hair, cut level with her pearl earrings, swing in time. Jane only stopped to tear the ball from her grip, using such force that the older woman was almost pulled off balance.

Shakily, with everyone staring at her, Jane went back to the bench, took Camilla's bag and hurried away and down the stairs.

Camilla was in a toilet on the first floor, bending over a wash basin with the hot water tap running. The room was dark apart from an illuminated Emergency Exit sign which bathed her face in a dull, greenish glow. When Camilla saw Jane, she pulled a paper towel from the dispenser and dried her face. Jane put her arm round the girl. Seen through the condensation on the mirror, they could have been mother and daughter.

'She's always like that,' Camilla said. Somehow, it was meant as an excuse.

As she stroked Camilla's back, Jane felt the warmth of the girl's body through the material of her leotard.

'I have to go back up,' Camilla said.

'No, you don't. Forget about it.'

Jane's hand slid upwards to a bony shoulder. She felt as if she were standing at the top of a dizzyingly tall staircase, holding on to the ball at the end of the handrail. She closed her eyes for a few seconds.

'You mustn't listen to that woman. You're very good.'

Camilla groaned as she threw the balled-up paper towel into the wire basket. She was ashamed by her poor performance and full of contempt for herself, just as the trainer had intended. The girl could not accept a compliment. Jane took a step back.

'You are, you know.' She breathed in, and the air seemed to have to force its way past various obstacles.

'Oh, yeah?' Camilla said and rolled her eyes.

A damp strand of hair dangled in front of her face. Jane pushed it back behind Camilla's ear and kept her hand there for just long enough to work out a more pedagogic way of approach.

'What is the goal you are all working towards?'

'To become champions of Europe.'

Her pronunciation of English was adorable and her minor syntactical errors only emphasized how much of a child there still is inside a fourteen-year-old.

'What is your chance of that?'

'If I work hard for two more years and the Bulgarian girls don't…'

Camilla avoided Jane's eyes in the mirror.

'I see. The idea is, you'll starve yourself for a couple more years and be bullied five times a week so that, maybe, you'll be a European champion of a uniquely weird sport?'

'I'm not starving myself.'

'So you say. But her pinching you, what was that for?' She almost ended the sentence with 'little Miss', a rhetorical habit from the days when she often discussed matters with a little Miss.

'I don't think she meant to pinch me.'

'Come on, I saw it. I'm sorry to have to say it but this outfit is an anorexia factory. There are little girls of nine up there who ought to be in hospital.'

Camilla smiled, a little superciliously.

'I really have to go back.'

Jane shook her head. She had already got the car keys out of her coat pocket and rattled them to show she was serious.

On the way home, Jane filled the silence with a discourse on what mattered in life and what one should not put up with, as a person and as a woman. To leave that place had been a grown-up, rational decision. Jane thought that there had been no other choice and would explain the situation to Eva. She would not escort the distraught girl back up that staircase; it was simply not an option. Jane was convinced that Eva had been pushing her daughter but could probably be forgiven for not having seen the light earlier, even though she had surely been aware of how the gym club operated. Camilla must have been training since she was about five years old, together with other girls whose parents also sanctioned with their silence the whole anti-cultural set-up. They had been sliding slowly into acceptance of an insane situation, as an outsider could see at a glance. Time for the blushing admission one has to make at least once in a lifetime: Yes, I see... now you put it like that, well...

Eva met them at the door. Camilla hurried away upstairs and her mother followed her.

'It became a bit tense,' Jane said.

Eva stopped halfway up the stairs. She had a skewed view of Jane through the sheet glass panels. Small muscles were visibly twitching at her jaw.

'Yes, thanks, I know already. I've been informed.'

'Informed?'

'The head coach phoned.'

'Doesn't she have just *the* most annoying voice?' Jane said.

But Eva was already taking the last steps of the stairs.

Jane went into the open-plan kitchen with her coat still on, poured herself a glass of water and drank in small sips while she supported herself with one hand on the counter. The room seemed unnecessarily brightly lit, like a kitchen exhibit in a trade fair. She thought about what to say next and, in her head, heard her own voice sound alternately regretful and self-justifying. Eva's judgemental streak constantly threatened to surface. As if she lived with an incurable disappointment, as if the world owed her something better. Jane asked herself if this might be a characteristic trait of Norwegian women. A travel writer with a talent for gross simplifications might just have put it all down to the climate. Or all that oil money. Perhaps Norwegian women collectively suffered from a bad conscience because they were sober people who had suddenly become rich?

She had started to shake again.

Eventually, Eva came downstairs. There were red spots on her forehead but her eyes were impassive as she went to stand behind the solid dinner table. Just beneath Jane's embarrassment and fear of losing control, she felt righteously exasperated on Camilla's behalf. How could it be defensible to make these girls keep going back to the gym? She thought of their fragile, unknowing bodies, their small ears exposed by the tightly pulled-back hairdos. How alone they surely were, these girls, although watched by their seated mothers? Camilla should not return to that place ever again. Jane felt that she had better close her eyes, in case her mouth said things her brain would rather it hadn't:

'Eva, I'm serious. Presumably you know what's going on in that place?'

The heat rash at Eva's hairline must be infectious.

'No. What is going on, Jane?' Eva asked calmly.

'What's going on? What *happens* there?'

'You tell me.'

'What happens…' Damn Eva's cunning, her fixed stare made Jane repeat herself. 'It is that… they remove the girls' self-confidence and replace it with… rhythmic gymnastics.'

Eva nodded as if getting the point.

'Honestly, they bully the girls.'

'And you worked all this out in one brief visit?'

'That's right, I did.'

'I see.' Eva went to the fridge, opened the door and pretended to be very preoccupied.

'What are you going to do?'

'Jane, right now I'm going to make supper.'

'So, you intend to carry on exposing Camilla to the gym sessions?' Jane had taken her coat off and realized that she was fussing about, trying to hang it up on the back of a chair.

'Whatever I do, I won't discuss it with you.' There was a long pause before Eva finally added, lowering her voice, 'To be absolutely frank, I'm not quite clear why you're here at all.'

Jane's hands went to her belly as if she had been knifed. Eva was still turned away from her, standing at the counter cutting up broccoli.

'You bitch,' Jane exclaimed.

She had lost control over what she said, just like her coat, still a bundle in her hands. And that first transgression of hers brought on more.

'I've noticed how you talk to Lars Christian sometimes, and to shop assistants and waiters as well. That prodding look of yours. "But, Lars Christian, I thought we had agreed that…"' She imitated Eva's sing-song tone of voice with its note of restrained aggression. To play-act was liberating. 'Oh, yes. "I have got it all, husband and kids and I know just precisely how I want it. I go jogging and then go jogging some more. And keep everyone in order and fetch and carry and drink a glass of red wine of an evening. Never more than one, God forbid."'

Eva had turned round now, her eyes shiny with disbelief. Jane asked herself if this was the time to put all her cards on the table. Hers was an unbeatable hand. She might choose to have a breakdown right here in the kitchen and melt into a sympathy-provoking mess. But she could not make herself do it.

Her body was quaking as she rushed into the hall, put on her trainers and pushed the door open with her shoulder while struggling with one sleeve of her coat. Polish Eva and her partner stood smoking outside under the recessed all-weather lamps lighting the porch. They stood where it was hard to pass them. Anyway, Jane had no idea where she wanted to go. She found a packet of cigarettes and a lighter in her coat pocket, and with darting movements, lit a cigarette and put it between her lips.

'Brr, it's getting cold.' Jane made it sound as if her trembling voice was just mimicry.

Neither replied. She smiled with, as she well knew, a wild look in her eyes.

'Isn't it cold in that trailer of yours?'

'No,' Eva said.

Presumably, if one travelled farther into Europe, one would eventually find a place where people communicated exclusively in tiny hand gestures to exchange goods and services, or to mate.

Later, after Jane had sneaked back upstairs to the guest room, she discovered the trap she was caught in. She had been fooled by the blister pack, as usual, pressed out what she needed for weeks while the treacherous silver foil had kept its shape and tricked her into thinking that she had several intact rows left. She straightened up and, with her hand pressed against her neck, looked out over the dark garden. She had been thinking about alcohol roughly every five minutes since she had driven Camilla to the gym and this, in turn, had triggered her need to check the stocks in her Valium cache.

Lars Christian was home now. She could hear his and Eva's voices from downstairs and a childish sensation came back: having to put up with adults talking about you, hearing them through walls and floor, using indistinguishable words; the child praying for forgiveness but mixing the words of the prayer with a mantra of impotent hatred. I hope they die. I hope they die.

Behind her closed eyes, she had a vision of a scorched landscape, grey and smoking as if after a firestorm. Over there, the ruins of the university where she had worked; and not far away, the remains of their house in Madison – nothing much left except the chimney, a charred writing desk and – as if it had been TV reportage – a child's soft toy lying in the ashes;

then, the sooty foundations of her parents' apartment by Lake Michigan – Robert and Dorothy using their hands to search the ashes. This was the America she had left behind. What had been ahead for her, on the other side of the ocean, was not necessarily a much greener place and, on the whole, faceless, but at least it did not burn.

A cautious knock on the door. She hoped it would be Camilla but it was Lars Christian's narrow face that appeared round the edge of the door.

'May I come in, Jane?'

It was a toothless question. He was obviously trying hard to be conciliatory. She had been told of the importance of 'cosiness' in this country.

She felt like saying: it's your home.

He made for the chair next to the bed and she had to move a small pile of underwear into the suitcase on the floor.

Lars Christian was smiling as his tired eyes fixed on her.

'She was upset that you, both of you rather, became a little hostile.'

Jane, for the first time, uttered a Norwegian-style *uhum*.

'She felt it really wasn't for you to be involved in… this. Your relationship with us still isn't… that close, even though it's very exciting from the point of view of our family history.'

Jane sat on the edge of the bed and made herself small. She was sorry for Lars Christian, whose role as messenger or negotiator seemed to be robbing him of more vestiges of masculinity. What was left disappeared swiftly with the words he had been charged to pass on. Jane noted that he didn't speak of *Eva* but of *she*.

'She has gone to bed now but in the morning…'

'First thing tomorrow morning, I'll apologize, Lars Christian. As soon as I see her.'

'That's good.'

She looked up at him with a question on the tip of her tongue but he got in first.

'I never felt this rhythm gymnastics thing was right for Camilla.' He spread his arms. 'But for as long as she enjoys it…'

For a moment, it occurred to her that she might be charmed by Lars Christian. In another life. Say, if he had been Camilla's sole carer. A compelling if fleeting thought came and went: bend forward, put your hand on his thigh, high up, do it now.

Lars Christian stood, ready to leave her room.

'You…' she said.

He stopped with his hand on the door handle.

'Lars Christian, if I need to consult a doctor here, how do I go about it?'

'I hope you're not unwell?'

'No, no. Or, to be precise…'

The information on the back of the box was mostly for epileptics, not people with conditions like hers.

'I'm an epileptic. It's not bad and usually well controlled. But I've run out of medicine.'

'I see.' Lars Christian slowly pushed the door handle down, then let it click back up again. 'I promise to call our doctor tomorrow morning. He will surely write out a prescription straight away. As long as you know exactly what you need.'

'Valium. Ten milligram tablets.'

Lars Christian repeated this.

'I'll get in touch with him as soon as I get into work tomorrow morning.'

During the night, the dream came back for the first time for weeks. As always, she dreamt that she had gone to Chicago for the Newberry seminar on American literary history and was in a hotel room when there was a knock on the door. With only small modifications, the dream dealt in real events as they had unfolded that morning in Chicago. It was more like a retelling of the past, without the nightmare's delirious lack of any logic or predictability, where rooms can change into other places. She had been sitting in an armchair with its back to the window. One curtain had been pulled back and the crisp light of dawn fell on a hotel writing pad in her lap. She had made a few last notes on the presentation she was to give later that morning on John Updike's literary legacy.

In the dream, as in reality, she assumed that a cleaner was waiting outside the door and it made her look for anything embarrassing left lying around. She had checked in late and had hardly had time to do more than take a few steps across the carpet. That morning, she had already tidied the bed a little and didn't need more towels.

As she walked the short distance to the door to tell whoever was outside that she was fine and busy with something important, she managed – in the dream, at least – to have a vision of her life with Greg and Julie, a distillation complete with an extremely concentrated run-through of moments of shame and happiness but also rich in detail, down to things like Greg's tone of voice when he told her that he wanted to take her surname (*a land of ashes is better than Noland at all*) and Julie's trembling lower lip when she had fallen from the climbing frame in Olin Park and, as they found out later, broken her arm.

There was another knock on the door, but by then she knew what to expect and didn't want to take the last few steps across the floor. It was at this point that the most marked discrepancies occurred: in the dream, the voice of the overweight woman police officer who had done the knocking did not come from *outside* the door; she was suddenly sitting at the end of Jane's bed in full uniform, and at her side stood a younger male colleague and the hotel manager who had escorted them. The policewoman cupped her hands to form a bowl that hid something from view. Her eyes attracted Jane, who slowly came closer, even though she realized that the hidden thing was something she didn't want to see.

'Jane Ashland? We must talk to you,' the hotel person said in an oddly tuneful voice, like a clarinet's.

The policewoman reached out her arms towards Jane, solemnly parting her hands as if to offer up a sacrifice or scatter petals. Reluctantly, Jane leant forward and saw, in the woman's palms, a small dead animal, its fur torn and bloody.

A sound out of hell woke her. She knew she must take something. Golden light filtered in through the gap beneath the blind. The colour made her think of organs stored in formaldehyde. She turned to lie on her front, raised the blind a little and saw the Poles busying themselves with an angle grinder just below her window. In a cloud of concrete dust, Andrej or Andrzej watched as Eva cut a flagstone in half.

In between the heart-wrenching howls, the house was quiet. Jane walked downstairs barefoot, still in her nightdress, holding her wallet in her hand. She crossed the terrace and then the lawn where the frost was shrinking back into the shadows under the thuja trees. The sun's rays bounced off the roof of the caravan and burned her corneas. She could have counted the blades of grass.

Eva looked up and saw Jane just as she was about to start cutting a new concrete slab. Jane covered her ears with the wallet and her free hand as she stepped inside the dust cloud, which smelt strongly of gunpowder. How easy it was to lose one's sense of reality when there was nothing else left to lose. When the grinding disc had stopped spinning, she made her face convey 'you know how one can feel sometimes' and asked if she could buy one of their bottles of vodka.

The young man grinned, as if in sympathy.

'No problem,' Eva mumbled.

Their reaction didn't surprise her. She had mentally granted them both a capacity for observation, a grasp of reality that the Askeland-Nilsens lacked. She had a vision of their lives, impoverished and bleak, among storm-lashed grey tower blocks in a former Soviet state – existences in which pretence had no place.

She mixed the vodka with some of the blackcurrant cordial she had found in the kitchen. The first glass went down quickly, the second she sipped as slowly as she could and remembered how Charles Bukowski had put it: 'When you drank, the world was still out there, but for the moment it didn't have you by the throat.' Though Bukowski had omitted to mention that after the third shot of alcohol, a sensation of suffocating could come back and, later still, of keeping barely a pace or two ahead of someone pursuing you down a dark alleyway.

At one point, she found herself in Camilla's room, sitting on the girl's bed with a large, yellow soft toy from IKEA squashed against her chest. Then, she threw up in the bathroom on the second floor and had to use the end of her toothbrush to push lumps of vomit down the washbasin drain holes. She showered for a long time and settled down in a cheerful mood to wait for the Askeland-Nilsens to come home. As the afternoon wore on, she had persuaded herself that the quarrel between herself and Eva was simply typical of what happened in an extended family. People occasionally would have different points of view. A bagatelle, then, rather like the matter of the damaged soap dish in the shower cubicle. She had knocked it down and hidden it deep inside the trash can.

By seven in the evening, no one had turned up. The Polish couple retreated into their trailer, leaving behind a numbing silence. She poured the last of the blackcurrant cordial into a mug with a measure of spirits and drank the lot leaning over the kitchen counter from where she could see the road through a low, narrow window.

Lars Christian's Volvo drove up at around eight o'clock. He parked near the wire fence outside the site as the last metres to the garage were still not flagged. Camilla climbed out slowly. She was wearing the white tracksuit and her hair was up. Jane thought her face had the same pained expression as after the training the other night, and ran out into the hall. As soon as she had stepped inside, Jane pulled Camilla close and pressed her lips against the girl's hair. Lars Christian's presence in the same space registered as a distracted gaze, minor movements, jackets being hung up. Camilla giggled a little and said something in Norwegian before slipping out of Jane's embrace and disappearing into the bathroom.

Lars Christian suddenly stopped in front her. He stood quite still. She focused on a point above his eyebrows.

'How has your day been?' she asked. What she actually wanted to know was if he had got hold of her medication. At the deep inlets in his hairline, his skin was tight and smooth. She wanted to put her finger up where his hair had once grown and follow the curve until it reached the first small, childishly downy hairs.

'I... well, I don't know. All right?' Lars Christian tried to catch her eye.

'This arrived today,' he said. He was holding a square cardboard box in his hand. 'Your book!'

'That was quick.'

'Express delivery apparently takes no more than two to four days.'

'All the way from the States?'

'Yes.'

She felt uncomfortable at the sight of the Amazon box, like a victim of blackmail confronting a box crammed with evidence of sins of the past.

'It's just a book,' she said.

Lars Christian looked confused, turned towards the shoe rack and finally let her pass.

She went back to the kitchen. Her empty mug had vanished from the draining board. She was positive that she had left it there after rinsing it. She heard Camilla and Lars Christian's voices from another room. The only word she understood was *shampoo*.

'Have you noticed that we're out of hot water?' Lars Christian asked. He had suddenly come in and stood behind her with the broken soap dish in his hand.

A small chunk of time had worked loose and dropped off without her noticing. The door to the dishwasher was open and the top rack pulled out.

'No, I haven't. Maybe they showered for too long?' She gestured towards the caravan in the garden.

Lars Christian looked at her until she turned back to the dishwasher.

'Eva has collected your medicine from the pharmacy. She'll be back soon.'

'Thank you!' Her intense relief made her take a small, silly dance step.

She closed the dishwasher lid and stood still, gripping the edge of the counter.

'I think I had better rest a little before she comes back,' she said, addressing Lars Christian's back. 'I feel a little off balance because I haven't taken my medicine.'

'Yes, of course.'

'Not that I get epileptic fits or anything,' she said cheerfully, imitating a few twitchy spasms as a child might, to mock the disabled.

Just as she crossed the threshold of the guest room and before she fell onto her bed, her writer's genes forced her for a brief moment to look at the whole scene from another angle: how bizarre it must be to have an intoxicated foreign woman, a complete stranger, staying in one's guest room.

She woke up because someone was looking at her. It was Camilla. She knocked gently on the open door and asked, 'Why is Oskar here?'

'Sorry?'

Camilla pointed towards something just by Jane's head. A perception as thin and sharp as the edge of a knife made her turn slowly round. Immediately in front of her eyes, the yellow toy from Camilla's room was lying on her pillow.

Camilla cautiously approached the bed, as if Jane were an animal likely to bolt any second.

'Mummy asked me to give you these.'

She placed an orange and white box of tablets on the edge of the bed. One word on it jeered at her in bold type: *rektal*. For rectal use only. Tight-lipped, she slumped back onto the pillow. Camilla asked if something was wrong.

'No, honey. Nothing at all.'

She closed her eyes, and then opened them again. Camilla was still standing there.

'Jane?'

'Yes,' she said, staring up at the ceiling.

'In your book. There was something printed inside. On one of the first pages.'

A long pause, and then it came.

'Who are Greg and Julie?'

*

Afterwards, parts of what had happened next had been wiped from her memory, as if by an act of charity. Regrettably, she could still recall that, around ten o'clock that evening, she was lying on her side trying to insert a Valium suppository when Martin, the son of the house, burst into the guest room to say hello to her.

She also remembered that Eva had asked if she was on something and that her own answer had consisted largely of the word 'insinuate', repeated insistently in a loud voice. And that she had been clinging to Lars Christian when Eva escorted her, carefully but with determination, to the front door. And that Camilla didn't cry, which Jane perhaps would have wished her to. She sat in the hire car outside the Askeland-Nilsen family home until dawn broke, since the one thing in the world she would never do was drive under the influence.

O N THE FIRST MORNING, they crossed the crystalline waters of a river and walked uphill through a forest about to lose its last glowing, autumnal tints. The slope was so steep that she was looking straight at the backs of Ulf's knees.

'Freak-show animals. That's all they're seen as. Tourist attractions. Because they're not native. Foreign introduction. If I had been researching wild reindeer, I'd have had an easier time of it. My own office. And so forth.'

Then he launched into a lecture on public funding of research and how it was administered, most of which Jane couldn't follow. But she did take on board that the train killed around ten musk oxen every year because the railway lines had been cut straight through their territory.

After a while, Ulf had drawn a bit ahead of her. The distance between them grew until he was out of sight. He waited for her farther up the ridge but as soon as she caught up, he set off again. The process, which was repeated many times, meant that he got some rest but she didn't.

'You'll tell me if I'm walking too fast, won't you?' Ulf said. And walked off and left her behind again.

After a few hours of this, they finally reached the plateau. The forest had ended at a line as sharp as if it had been the edge of a tilled field. They stood there for a while. The expanse around them was absolutely still. So much solid mass: you would expect it to produce some kind of sound. A vast number of stones of all sizes lay immobile in the feeble sunlight. The path continued across other ridges until details were lost in the distance. The eye could just make out, even farther away, contrasts of black and white on a faultless peak.

'Isn't it fantastic?'

It was. To say the least.

'I feel so incredibly alive up here, at one with nature,' Ulf went on.

Jane searched for traces of irony in his face but his eyes didn't leave the snowy mountain top. He kept looking at it as he moved close to her and put his arm round her shoulders.

'Up here is a perfect place for recharging one's batteries.'

She giggled and felt at the same time a pang of loneliness that reached into the core of her body. It made her think about the first boy she'd slept with, a guy called Ray Dechamps, whom she had been told was a catch, partly because his older brother drove a Pontiac with flame-effect paintwork on the hood.

Ulf let his hand stay on her shoulder. There was a stack of flattish stones just next to them.

'Why have the stones been put on top of each other?' she asked.

'It's a cairn,' Ulf told her.

'What's a cairn?'

'A marker to show where the path is.'

'But the ones over there are quite far from the path.' She pointed.

'True.'

'So why are they there?'

'People build them.'

'Why do?...'

Ulf made a tut-tut noise and started walking.

For a few seconds, Jane stood quite still with her eyes closed. Then she followed him. Low pale green shrubs that reminded her of wormwood or sage brushed against her trouser legs and covered previously made trails.

The path took them high up the side of a valley with a shallow river running far below. The shimmering mist from the river hung in the air like a spider's web. Jane caught up with Ulf and walked alongside him. She began talking about something she hadn't planned to talk about – something she felt was over and done with. But then, it might be the kind of thing Ulf would approve of, what with his going on about being one with nature.

'One might begin to wonder if there isn't something that is bigger than us.'

She spread her arms wide.

'Like what?'

'Perhaps something that exists outside or beyond the individual.'

'You don't express yourself very clearly,' Ulf said, staring straight ahead.

'I listened to a highly regarded physicist doing one of the TED Talks and he was arguing that all systems possess a level of consciousness, and the more complex the system, the more advanced the consciousness. One possible consequence of his argument is that there is an enormous, superior consciousness.'

'God?'

Ulf said the word in a way that made it sound anaesthetizingly dull.

'Not necessarily. But some force in nature, something large and powerful that our empiricism has not yet helped us to discover.' She almost had to run to keep up with him and her voice trembled. 'Something we've perhaps avoided taking notice of, and preferred to put into a religious category?'

'Instead of what?'

'What that physicist was talking about.'

She had always been more persuasive, and sounded wiser, in writing than in speech. The discrepancy had long frustrated her and that frustration had been one of the factors that made her decide to be a writer when she was just twelve or thirteen years old. When she became a teacher, she prepared herself so thoroughly that the lessons mostly entailed reciting her own texts from memory.

Ulf stopped abruptly, looked quickly around, and then bent down to pull something off from where it grew on the side of a stone.

'Look at this!' he said, pointing to a tuft of moss.

'Where?'

'Just there.'

She looked closer. The tip of his index finger was indicating a pale, trumpet-shaped growth a little larger than the head of a pin.

'Look at its perfect shape!'

It reminded her of the rough horns of plenty that children used to draw in school for Thanksgiving.

'Cladonia fimbriata, or trumpet lichen. Belongs to the class of Lecanoromycetes. This is one of the wonders of nature. No need to look any further for wonderfulness. I can tell you exactly how it originated and why it grows in this habitat.'

'I don't doubt that at all.'

Ulf threw the moss away. She had expected him to return it to the stone reverently, which would, one way or the other, have supported the point he had made.

Then he raised the binoculars that hung round his neck, placed his legs well apart and started turning slowly.

'Musk oxen are harder to spot in the autumn when the heather has turned brown.'

She considered using her binoculars, too, but they were in the bottom of her rucksack.

'Because the musk oxen are brown as well,' Ulf added.

'I get it,' Jane said.

He was reaching the end of a panoramic scan carried out evenly and methodically, and didn't seem bothered when the binoculars pointed straight at her face.

'Do you see anyone?' she asked.

'No one,' he said.

When they stopped the first night, Ulf walked down to a mountain stream that had carved a gully in the ground behind their campsite. A good-sized gully, but not deep enough to leave it in any doubt that he was naked. Afterwards, he went over to her and stood in full view with a tiny, green microfibre towel as a loincloth. He was in great shape and almost certainly noticed that she noticed.

Jane started to pull the tent out of its bag.

'Is that a tattoo you've got there?' Jane asked.

Ulf came closer and contracted one pectoral muscle.

'It symbolizes freedom,' he said.

The tattoo showed an eye.

'It's an eagle's eye. I've always been interested in eagles.'

'Isn't everyone?'

'But I figured having an entire eagle would be a little banal, so just the eye seemed a better idea.'

'How's one to know that it's the eye of an eagle? Not the eye of a budgie, say?'

'How does one know?' His eyebrows moved a little higher up. He drew a small circle on his chest muscle.

'You knew from the prominent shadow here, almost like an eyebrow.'

She leant closer to him.

'Boo!' he shouted and pressed his chest against her face. 'The eagle attacks!'

She had made up her mind to erect her tent, say that she was very tired, which happened to be true, too, and crawl into her sleeping bag at once. While Ulf got dressed, she dragged the inner and outer sheets, the tent pins and an unlikely number of lengths of rod out of the olive-green tent bag. Naturally, there was no set of instructions. In Norway, anything to do with tents was supposed to be common knowledge.

While she struggled with the tent, she sensed Ulf observing her.

'Jane. About those books of yours?'

He was stirring a bagful of freeze-dried food. It was the first time he had shown any interest in her work – or, what *had been* her work.

'What kind of novels are they?'

'I don't know what to say… just, novels.'

She hadn't meant to sound curt but his question was one she had always found difficult to deal with. She stood still, a piece of tent rod in each hand, and thought about *The Age of Plenitude*. She had written it as if she still lived in the time before the September 11 attacks, before the economic crisis. While other writers had taken on board the seriousness of the times, she had carried on focusing on smaller causes and effects. But why shouldn't she? Her world had not changed. She didn't know many people who had lost their jobs, and *no one* who had died when the Twin Towers collapsed. Presumably, many readers had been in the same situation, since the book sold so well. But the sales could also reflect a need for escapism, something similar to the seventies pop tune 'Happy Times' shooting to the top of the music charts in the middle of the grimmest recession since the Great Depression.

Besides, what she wrote was not easy-going or far from real life. She wrote about unrequited love, social anxiety, weariness. And she had tackled such themes again in her last manuscript. It was never completed. She had reached page 104 of the story about a woman who had a comfortable life with uncomplicated existential challenges until the all-powerful Author decided it was time for some high seriousness and an old, cold metal arm swung down from Heaven and flattened her under a full stop.

'I read mostly professional stuff,' Ulf said.

'Of course, it makes sense.'

She had managed to slot two equally long rods together.

'But when I read fiction, I like a good story. Preferably with new subjects to learn about. You know, like historical events. Do you write about historical events?'

'I don't write any more, you know that.'

'But when you did, was it about history?'

'No, it wasn't.'

'What are your books about, then?'

She shrugged.

'A book must be about something, surely?'

'Must it? Can't it be about lack of action? Like *Seinfeld*.'

'I don't like *Seinfeld*.'

Yet another difference between them that, for a few long seconds, she allowed to grow into a huge, all-encompassing sense of loneliness.

'Are you sure you know what to do? Can I help?' he asked.

She had managed to insert several of the rods into place and had pulled the tent into an arch that looked completely unsafe.

'You concentrate on your tent and leave me to mine,' Jane said.

'My own tent?'

'That's right.'

'I didn't bring a tent. Now that we've got yours.'

The next day, fog was beginning to well up from the bottom of the valley. She trudged along behind Ulf again but the walking was tougher now. As the day wore on, it grew harder to share his enthusiasm about the many sightings of musk ox excrement. Maybe the tension that was growing between them had something to do with this. Her lack of interest in turds.

He walked with his chest thrust forward and his arms swinging vigorously, as if wading through deep water. Suddenly he exclaimed, 'And then they come along and tell me that I won't have access to the biodiversity labs. Top priority for phylogenetic systematology and evolution, if you please.'

She had no idea who *they* were and wasn't too sure about *phylogenetic* either. But in one way at least, all that was still within her field: the correct term for what Ulf had been saying is *egocentric speech*, a survival from an early phase in children's speech development. At that stage, the child doesn't recognize any clear boundaries between itself and the outside world, and doesn't take into account that it might have information that isn't available to whoever is listening.

There was another possibility, namely that Ulf had continued a line of thought he had been holding forth about but which she had missed because she had been walking just behind his back.

'He stole my boot when we were playing fire truck so I peed on the roof,' Jane said in a low voice.

But Ulf didn't register that she had said anything.

Before they had finished erecting the tent, the wind was back and the fog too. She used to think that wind and fog couldn't occur at the same time, that the two meteorological phenomena were mutually exclusive. How long could weather like this continue? Ulf didn't say. But the truth was: for days on end.

They were sitting in her tent drinking coffee when Ulf suddenly put his arm around her and pulled her close.

'We'll find them soon,' he said.

She hadn't taken any medicine since they left Dombås, even though a doctor there had let her have two whole boxes – and not suppositories either. Up here, she felt there was more room for her senses, letting them reach out freely into a world of nothingness. But her abstinence and the thickening mist combined into a feeling that reminded her of being young and having a migraine in a totally quiet bedroom on a Sunday afternoon. Ulf's arm around her waist seemed to hold her inside that feeling.

She caught the reflections in his glasses as his lips searched for hers. She turned away, not in conscious, thought-out rejection of him but instinctively, as one instantly wipes cobwebs off one's face while moving about in a dark attic. She had visualized the two of them kissing and even, at times and for whatever reason, wished that they would. But it felt quite different now, when it was about to happen.

She crawled out of the tent. Wandering off anywhere wasn't an option because the white-out had obliterated the landscape. She used up five matches to light a cigarette. When she glanced over her shoulder, she saw that Ulf was still inside the tent, lying on his belly and making notes in a spiral-bound notepad.

'I just wanted to see them standing in a circle,' she said loudly enough to be heard above the wind.

Ulf made a lot of noises intended to communicate strong feelings.

'You didn't think we would actually do that? You didn't think we would try to provoke that behaviour?'

Even with her back turned, she could sense Ulf shaking his head.

'Perhaps it hasn't struck you that it would be a dangerous thing to do? Indicated, for instance, by the words *defensive formation?*'

Admittedly, she hadn't considered this. Not in her state of Musk Ox aquavit-induced delirium that first evening. Nor at any time later. It had only been an image in her mind: animals in a circle.

'This summer alone, the air ambulance service had to pick up two tourists who hadn't observed the recommended safe distance.'

She threw the cigarette butt into a gust of wind and watched as it shot away like a small projectile.

'Musk oxen can get to sixty kilometres an hour at full speed,' Ulf pointed out.

Kilometres an hour was pretty meaningless to her, and she must have been visibly unimpressed because Ulf added, 'Usain Bolt can get to thirty-seven kilometres an hour over a short distance.'

'Perhaps he'd run faster if he was chased by a musk ox?'

Ulf turned back to his notes.

'Are there no warning signs?' she asked.

Ulf said while carrying on with his work, 'When they feel provoked, they start snorting and striking the ground with their horns.'

'Fine.'

'No, it's very much not fine,' Ulf said. 'Don't believe that these behaviours are kind of optional. One thing always follows another.'

She looked like a weary question mark.

'Imagine a large ship that's about to move away from the quayside. Two warning blasts and they're not saying: I might or might not be reversing now.'

'True. They mean: Out of my way!'

'Correct, Jane. But you don't usually move at sixty kilometres an hour, do you? At least, I haven't seen anything of the sort.'

'Fuck you, Ulf.'

'And you, Jane.'

J ULIE WAS ELEVEN. She used to say especially pleas-
ing words inside her head. Sometimes, when she thought
she was alone, the words became just audible, like whistling
with cracked lips: Engelbert Humperdinck. Hang Seng in
Hong Kong.

Julie filled the window sill in her room with tubes of fla-
voured lipgloss.

Julie became sarcastic when her blood sugar level was low.

Julie played the piano with the straight back of a piano-
playing girl of long ago.

Julie sat in the back of the car and let off a loud, bleating
burp and said, 'Oh dear. I'm so sorry.' Looking at her in the
rear-view mirror, it was obvious that a miraculous rebalancing
was underway: the size of her front teeth and her mouth was
more in keeping, her head was no longer a ball balanced on
the stick-like body of child.

Julie, all of her four feet eleven inches, curled up in your
arms and breathed warmly into your ear.

Julie laughed a lot.

Julie cried a lot.

Some of Julie's traits had jumped several generations: the
Miss Teen looks of her father's mother, the dark-blond hair of

an Askeland woman who left the poverty of Norway behind in the nineteenth century.

Julie was pernickety.

Julie swept her ponytail up high, pushed some hair forward to make a short fringe and mimicked a callow boy: 'Do you love me unconditionally?'

Julie danced as if she were the only one alive in the world.

Now and then, Julie was allowed to choose her own clothes: jeans that looked as if they'd been painted on her legs, tops that left her belly bare. Frills! It was impossible to work out if her choices were alarmingly sexualized or if the alarmist adult gaze added that special charge.

Julie was eleven but slept as if she were an infant, one hand protectively against her neck. Greg whispered, 'Remember, she did that even at St. Mary's?'

Of all that Jane remembered from that time, her most distinct memory was the light. A light, as if painted in oils, was there every time she woke. Light falling on the roofs of the houses, snow-covered even though it was March, flowing in through the family room's two tall windows whose blinds could be raised electronically using a remote control so that, from her bed, Jane could regulate them according to how much light her heart could hold.

She lay there looking at Julie, after having been through a world of pain so implausibly overwhelming that she was already well on her way to forgetting it. Instead, there were Julie's domed, gummed-up eyes below little bumps that would, with time, grow into her eyebrows. And Julie's nose, no larger than the tip of Greg's little finger but still the most outgoing feature in a face that shouted: *Get me back in there where I came from!* In an instant, Jane realized that her own inner darkness was not the same as her own mother's, and that she would never come to prioritize her own emotional needs over the needs of this child. Although she had hardly talked to a child since she was one herself and thought her friends' children, despite appearing to be imitation human beings, were actually small trolls whose goal was to block all decent conversation, she found it very easy to love her own daughter. Watching Julie, Jane felt herself becoming the light, as if at any moment she might change from being a person into no more than the radiance illuminating her baby's face.

Among the mass of information made available to her before the birth – the Lamaze classes, the women's magazine articles, the pregnancy check-ups – nothing had been said about this light. All the factual knowledge, so much more than one could possibly wish for, was nothing but a cover-up for everyone's failure to describe it.

The staff at St. Mary's circled around them, offering every kind of postnatal support. Jane didn't respond with her usual edginess to gentle-voiced professional insistence, not even when a woman with large glasses and a floral blouse introduced her-self as *lactation consultant* and told her that she, the consultant, was available on a special *white phone line* so that Jane could air her breastfeeding issues at any time. Jane's urge to categorize, to distance herself, to resist – all was calmed by the light. This became very obvious when Robert and Dorothy visited. She listened smilingly to her mother's advice and interpreted her father's lack of engagement as just awkwardness (he stood by the window and argued about access to parking).

As parents they were novices, and shameless with it. The first time Greg did Julie's diapers, she was lying safely on a changing table with high edges but he still carried out the whole procedure with one hand while keeping his other hand gently on the baby's chest.

'She won't levitate,' Jane said.

'How do you know?' Greg said.

He took the next day off: sneaked out of his office at the *Wisconsin State Journal* after dashing off some copy for the entertainment pages, and battled his way past a multiple car crash on Beltline Highway, all in order to get to the hospital before the end of the evening. Jane had been struggling to stay awake and had to force her head out of her dream world to be kissed by Greg.

'On the way up, I met a hospital clown in the lift,' Greg told her.

'You did what?' she said in a voice still muffled by sleep.

'The hospital clown. I was chatting with him in the lift.'

'Why?'

'Why not?'

Then Greg grew quiet. She settled back into the bed and closed her eyes.

'Seems he wondered when we'd have time to see him,' he added.

'Are we to see him?' she mumbled.

'Oh, yes. He was emphasizing how important it is to lay the foundations of a humorous mindset at an early stage.'

'Gosh!'

'Yup,' Greg said and breathed in, as he always did in the middle of explaining something. 'I think the idea is rather like the skin-on-skin programme at St. Mary's but more focused on the newborn's social skills.'

She sat up in bed and rubbed her eyes.

'Well, maybe tomorrow, unless you have to...'

Then she discovered that Greg was beside himself with suppressed laughter and reached out across the bedside table to smack him.

Her bed was in the so-called family room, but Greg wasn't allowed to stay the night. There were no set visiting hours, but late at night a change in atmosphere somehow communicated to the visitors that the mothers would soon be due for a period of whispering peace. She wanted Greg to stay all the time and he didn't want to leave them. He held Julie close to his chest. His hair was still almost shoulder-length – that, and his tattoos, signified his last stand against becoming a grown-up and a career journalist – and as he bent his head over Julie to inhale her scent, father and daughter disappeared behind the dark curtain of his hair.

'Cruelty to children is impossible to understand,' Greg said in a low voice.

There was enough space in his hand for Julie's foot. Julie's toenails fascinated her parents perhaps more than any other part of her. They were so tiny it seemed out of order not to believe in God.

'I used to regard images of suffering children as a hackneyed media device. Now, I'm glad I'm writing about culture rather than working on the news desk,' Greg said. 'I start crying now every time I see suffering children on TV.'

'Do you, truly?'

'Last time was yesterday,' Greg said and swallowed.

He hesitated before starting to speak again. 'Imagine, my father beat me up.'

Greg still sounded as if it had happened recently. He had told her about his boyhood while they were still in New York. Mainly, the punishments had amounted to little more than slaps on the behind. Once, when Jeff went outside in a blizzard wearing only his pyjamas and Greg locked him out, a wire clothes hanger had been used.

'How come it's possible?' Greg demanded in a choked voice. 'What I mean is… the entire system of parental rule. Kids were hangers-on. Parasites, with restricted rights. We didn't have any say. Ran our childish world according to our own system. And it mustn't clash at any time with the much more important adult world.'

'True,' she said.

'Of course, it was still worse to be a child in the fifties when our parents were growing up. Not to speak of the childhoods our grandparents had to put up with!'

The blanket slipped from Greg's arm. Jane wrapped it round Julie again.

'For instance, historians believe that Adolf Hitler was economical with the truth in *Mein Kampf* when he describes his father's brutality. It was probably much worse. You wouldn't credit it but this was the time when an Austrian expert pedagogue recommended hitting babies hard, for no reason – except to toughen them up!'

'Greg, why are we talking about Hitler?'

'I don't know.'

She pulled Greg close and kissed him. She felt that they both had softer, warmer lips than before. But then Greg backed away and continued stubbornly. 'No, I do know. The answer is: because I want us to do it differently. To be another kind of parent.'

And so they were. Jane and Greg felt that they belonged to the first generation of parents who regarded their children as complete human beings, held them in correspondingly high regard and thought so hard about their role that they were in a state of constant confusion. But the light never faded; it was like a flame that lit up days and nights. They had changed. Still, Jane was wrong to believe that the outside world would have changed, too. It caused just as many problems as ever and now there was a new source: Julie.

During Julie's childhood, Jane found herself going through compulsive rituals when no one was watching. There was a special time just before she fell asleep next to Greg. She saw things in her mind: steep stairways, a butcher's knife near the edge of the kitchen counter, the rusty bracket on a swing in the park. Such images forced her to reach out with her hand in the darkness to knock on the bedside table. In case Greg hadn't gone to sleep, the movement had to be disguised as fumbling for something on the table but must also be completed to fit the proverb: the knocking finger must touch wood. This often meant that the hand pretending to look for, say, the mobile charger, had to move a box of tissues or a magazine to get at the actual table top.

She pondered the borderline between superstition and compulsion. The ancient human need that led people to convince themselves that there was a system where none existed. The lengths to which people would go to make believe they could control the universe. She also wondered about how many others went in for behaviours like hers. Perhaps men and women everywhere in the USA were lying awake in bed at night, knocking on bedside tables, quickly switching the light on and off (if they were alone), clapping or snapping with their fingers under the covers, or hitting their hip bone rhythmically while saying: don't let it happen, don't let it happen, don't let it happen. All this, to save the one they loved.

As time went by, Jane became aware that her daughter could enrage her so much that she said and did things she would later regret bitterly. As it happened, these things were often said or done just when Julie was about to be left with her babysitter, or when Jane was going away for several days, which meant that she remained in a state of anguished self-reproach until she could once more hug her daughter tight and have the chance to make it up to her. On her way home from literary events and book readings, she would jump into taxis, zigzag across the airport to avoid business travellers and overweight tourists from the Midwest, drive all the way home in the left-hand lane on the highway, taking the corner of Spooner Street and Regent Street on screaming tyres – only to be told by Greg that Julie had just fallen asleep.

Julie was eleven when Jane realized that one of her rather slim novels was receiving unexpectedly enthusiastic attention. Greg called it *a great breakthrough*, but that was of course an exaggeration. *The Age of Plenitude* was in every way as demanding as her earlier books and as focused on language. Even so, it sold more copies than all her previous titles put together. Her editor said that was because it was *so fucking excellent*. Jane thought, although she kept it strictly to herself, that the cover had done the trick: it showed a woman on a beach just before the trend that placed woman-on-a-beach images in a special category of successful cover designs. She celebrated Greg's fortieth birthday, luckily more than a year before her own, by buying him an eighteen-foot fishing boat, a trailer and all available accessories for sport fishing. She joined him on trips a couple of times because she wanted to experience his happiness at being on board next to a cooler stocked with bottles of beer and an echo sounder display of flickering pixels, which might or might not be fish. Greg's most faithful companion on fishing trips was none other than Tom Belotti, Jane's admirer when they were at school. Tom had also moved to Madison and eventually become an especially good friend to both of them. He had married a Russian nurse with nearly transparent teeth, who could look about seventeen one moment and fifty-five the next. You were asked to believe a backstory about Vladlena (what joy, just to say her name…) that involved a wild party at the Russian embassy and a love that conquered every barrier of language and culture placed in its way. This story was about as credible as young Tom's tale about the white shark that lived in the filter system of the public swimming pool in Brookfield and was let out for exercise a couple of times a year. Tom had spotted Vladlena for the first time in an online catalogue of Russian women wanting to marry. But they seemed happy together.

The unexpected success of Jane's latest book spurred her on. She wanted to work harder, write more and faster, speed up her publication rate, say yes to invitations, and generally carry on doing whatever was needed to make a name for herself because there seemed to be a genuine interest in what she was writing – she no longer felt that to be a writer meant holing up in some dark cubbyhole and making stuff up. On the days she didn't teach at the university or attend some event out of town, she typed away on a new novel. She could hear when Julie came through the door after school, but more and more often just called out a greeting from her upstairs study; the front door seemed to open in the middle of the most important sentence so far. During the frenetic hours before Greg came home, her conscience was always on its way to Julie. She had been an only child herself and knew just what the tense quietness downstairs meant.

One Thursday at the beginning of May, Jane felt she needed to meet Julie after school and spend a few hours with her before she had to go to the weekly hour of piano playing with Mrs Gurzky (this was a Greg project). Jane's longing had an urgency she hadn't felt since Julie was very young. She must save what she had written and hurry out. Later, this appeared to be a portent, a sign so unmistakable that, in her capacity as creative writing instructor, she would have called it *foreshadowing*.

Probably, her longing had sprung from three recent events. For one thing, a few days earlier, Julie had preferred to be driven to a friend's house rather than going with her mother to buy a new swimsuit, a choice Jane saw as confirmation of her daughter's growing independence. Secondly, Jane was off to the Newberry seminar in Chicago the following day, and had to spend several days without seeing Julie. Thirdly, she had drunk so much coffee throughout the morning that her brain seemed to lay exposed and trembling, like a dish of jelly on a picnic table.

In the handout on 'Safe Delivery and Collection', parents were told to park behind the tall fence around the yard on the western side of the school. However, Julie would come out through the main entrance on the opposite side of the building. Jane squeezed the car up against the kerb on Chadbourne Avenue, along with other parents who either felt like irresponsible slobs or actually were. While she waited in the car for the clock to show 2.37pm, the eccentric end point of the school day at Randell Elementary, she was cross with herself for not collecting Julie more often. It was always Greg who played with her and Jane who helped with dull homework; Greg who joined in ball games and Jane who cooked complicated Mediterranean food with a glass of Chablis in her hand. She couldn't understand why she hadn't taken pleasure in things like sitting on the floor with Julie and fussing with the nylon hair, bristling with static electricity, of a small, plastic pony.

When Julie and her friends came out of school, Jane was brimming with coffee-induced expectation. She had rolled down the car window but managed to hold back from shouting. This was how Julie looked when she didn't know her mother was watching her: whispering and whooping, dancing about in tight jeans, knock-kneed when she giggled. Jane recalled this moment of childhood: the taste of eraser in her mouth, multicoloured nylon bags dangling from thin shoulders, the way one had to swing one's hair out of the way of the straps, the yelling and squeaking of sneakers on a stone floor becoming a mass of sound that built behind her, higher and higher until she was ejected through the door and the sound turned into rustling in the treetops.

They drove along Lake Monona. Julie was in the back. No one seems to know exactly when a child is old enough to sit in front. The grass was green along the water's edge but the bleakness of winter lingered in the lake and the sky above. Julie was deep into one of her long tales about an episode from her school day, something Amy had said to Joe just at the moment Joe was tipping forwards and back on his chair so that the teacher was just... and he just, and then she just... Jane watched in the mirror as the eagerness to tell bubbled in the corners of Julie's mouth, nodded and agreed when it seemed appropriate, but was aware that, in her head, she was inside the scene she had been working on before leaving her study.

'Mom?'

Jane often reflected on how she would like to have about three hours to surface after being immersed in her fictions, something like the pressure equalization that divers need.

'Mom?'

'Yes?'

'Where are we going?'

'I thought it might be a good idea to go look for that swimsuit.'

'OK. But Dad and I have already been looking online.'

She switched the blinker on with excessive force as she changed lanes.

'So, what's the upshot? Do you need a swimsuit or don't you?'

Julie didn't answer for a while, then: 'I don't.'

'Terrific!'

The rush of coffee had squeezed the blood out of her fingers.

Julie sat gazing at the water. Her lips were moving slowly.

'Are you tired?' Jane asked carefully. It actually meant *I am tired, just so you know.*

And Julie knew. She shook her head.

Jane took it further and said in a fluting voice, 'Well then, we'll have time for a little stroll in the botanic garden, won't we?'

'Why?' Julie had earned the right to a little resistance.

'It's so lovely at this time of year.'

Julie turned to look out through the window.

'Can we phone Dad?'

'Of course.'

Jane tried to reach behind her back to hand over her cell and almost dislocated her shoulder. The pain felt so up-to-date somehow.

'Julie! Come on, take it.'

'Oh.'

When Greg answered, he seemed to be inside a cardboard box together with the entire editorial staff.

'Dad, you're on loudspeaker.'

'Hiya, is that you?'

'We're in the car.'

'Wait, let me…'

A drawn-out, scraping noise, then silence at last.

'There. Welcome to the copier room. What are you up to?'

'We're going to the botanical garden,' Julie said. 'It's so lovely at this time of year.'

Thanks, Julie, Jane thought.

'Jane? Are you there?'

'I'm driving the car.'

'Do you know what Clive said?' Greg asked rhetorically.

They were driving through a tunnel. Jane and Julie stretched their necks like alert animals.

'He said from now on, there will be fewer feature articles. They're no longer prioritized. Just as I thought,' Greg continued. 'What did you say to that?'

'That I don't give a shit because I have a boat that's perfect for perch fishing. With a rotating chair on deck.'

'Julie is here too, in case you had forgotten.'

'Says *you?*'

Compared to Greg, she had always been poor at controlling her speech in their daughter's presence. She might make rude comments about strangers within Julie's hearing. *Why don't you just jog off? You look like it'd do you good.* She had asked herself if, by sharing her bad as well good sides, she was trying to get closer to Julie as she grew older. *Best of luck! You'll need it, with that hairstyle.* Would she become the kind of mother who hung out with her daughter in the mall, both in matching pink hoodies?

There was just one other car in the parking lot in front of the grounded spaceship that was the Bolz Conservatory. Between the pillars at the main door, an older man stood, pointing at a sign that blocked the entrance to the greenhouses. He seemed deeply disappointed.

Jane rolled the window down.

'Closed for emergency repairs,' quoted the man. He spoke so loudly she had to retreat from the window.

She thanked him, drove on and shouted to Julie in an old man's cracked voice, 'Under repair! Closed!'

There, she had done it again.

She suggested that they go for a walk in the open garden and the arboretum instead. Once more, Julie asked: why? And got the answer: why not? Julie climbed out of the car slowly and walked a few paces behind Jane across the parking lot. Jane felt that her day of sitting at her desk had left her bursting with pent-up energy. Walking along the gravelled track leading to the Perennial Garden, they found themselves inside the dust stirred up by a noisy ride-on lawnmower. The gardens were either bleakly black or flowering desperately.

They arrived at the grassy slope where outdoor concerts were held during the summer. An empty Coke can was lying on the lawn and she could see that Julie was tempted to give it a kick. Impulsively, Jane ran to beat her to it. Julie stopped in her tracks, gave off a subdued howl and started running. Jane had already reached the can and sent it across the grass in a fine arc. As they ran side by side to catch up with it, Jane managed to bump her hip into Julie's side to gain ground but Julie came back with a mean leg-hook that tripped Jane up. Lying on the ground, she got hold of a sneaker that had come off and threw it after Julie, who avoided a direct hit with one graceful sideways move, picked the shoe up and threw it among the pillars at the far end. Jane had to hobble along, shouting in annoyance. In front of her, Julie, very pleased with herself, was dribbling with the can. When Jane had got close enough, she took aim at Julie's thin ankles and lunged.

They both rolled about on the grass, trying to reach the can. Jane's foot was closest but Julie lay on top of her and pushed her elbow into Jane's thigh.

'I give in!' Jane cried.

'Loser.'

Afterwards, they went to the Thai Pavilion and compared the greenish stains on their clothes. Julie eagerly went through a blow-by-blow account of the battle and Jane, who was looking at her daughter's face, made the right noises to show that she was just as keen to relive the drama. Julie's eyes were very wide, her nose was wrinkled, her lips moved ceaselessly. All this attracted Jane's gaze, as did something else, both there and not there, that made her able to sense the shape of the young woman's mind. The old saying that *your child is only on loan* annoyed her: Julie was her daughter and, just as irrevocably, she was Julie's mother. No facile philosophizing could change that.

She thought she might write about the episode, turn it into a scene in a novel or perhaps a short story, but realized it wasn't a good idea. These moments had no intrinsic structure, no problematic issue, no conflict. Only love.

While they sat there, the big lawnmower rolled past them on the cobbles below the pavilion. The man was relaxed in his seat, steering with one finger on the wheel. He got to where the path branched on either side of a statue of a lion and, just before he might have disappeared behind the trees, he pulled a lever by his seat and swung the mower onto a grassy verge that ran parallel with the path. Jane watched with a vague sense of satisfaction as the rotating cutters created a lighter strip in the grass. Suddenly, a squirrel leapt out of a bush and ran straight at the machine. Julie had her back turned and didn't notice Jane's gasp. The squirrel tried a few pointless escapes, jumping first to one side, then to the other, before it vanished under the blades. The man obviously hadn't seen it. Jane held her breath while looking past Julie at the mower. When the squirrel emerged from underneath it, she thought at first that it had survived intact because it moved so quickly. It kept jumping up and down, as if the ground were red hot. Then she understood: the squirrel had been mutilated and the jumping was the effect of an instinctive flight response. A healthy leg kicked out and sent the body high up in the air where it somersaulted and fell back, landing on its side or its head or one of its damaged limbs. A hard-wired sequence; one could hear the processor spin.

The mower followed the curving path out of sight. The squirrel was still making its terrible leaps but had shifted sideways onto the cobbles and there was a noise each time it hit the ground. Jane faced Julie with a big, shaky grin but it was too late – Julie had already turned round to see what it was. In the short moment Julie needed to take in the strange sight, Jane had time to imagine a scenario: she had to hold the kicking, struggling squirrel in one hand while prodding it to get a grip and break its little neck as an act of mercy.

Initially, Julie shocked her by laughing.

'Look! What is it *doing*?' Julie pointed.

But then, if Jane hadn't watched the whole sequence, she would probably have been just as baffled. Could they get away so easily? With luck, maybe the animal would bounce into the bushes, leaving her alone with a memory that would make her tell herself that 'nature must take its course', repeat it in the car on the way home and in bed before she fell asleep – but what nature? The kind of nature in which squirrels are carved up by lawnmowers?

No such luck.

'Mom, it's bleeding,' Julie cried.

Jane ran after her, past a small, concreted-in pond set in the space in front of the pavilion. Clouds moved swiftly across its still surface. Somehow it was as if she had never left her desk, as if she were still inside an imagined world. The closer they got to the squirrel, the more strongly she experienced its suffering as it shot up in the air and fell back, again and again. And with it, the realization that it wasn't even smart enough to put its pain into context. She knew Julie felt more or less the same. Jane had had to accept that empathy was probably not part of the human inheritance; she and Greg had been doling it out in regular doses, like teaspoons of medicine, throughout Julie's childhood. But by now, the medication had done its work and Julie was ready to suffer with all and everyone.

'Mom, do something!'

They stopped on the edge of the large, virtual circle surrounding the convulsing squirrel, Jane holding her arms protectively in front of her body while her hands attempted to mimic sensible things to do. They both turned away, repulsed, unable to watch, then forced themselves to look, screaming in unison.

And then it was all over. The squirrel lay still, its white belly up and its front paws folded.

Jane wanted the whole thing to be over and done with as soon as possible. She would have flicked the squirrel into the bushes with a stick, but suggesting it made Julie wail. Instead, Jane had to pick it up and carry it in her hands all the way through the park. She had thought it would be like picking up a kitten, but the wrecked little creature rested on her palms like an oozing bag of skin.

On the way home, the squirrel lay on the rubber mat between Julie's feet. The girl was beside herself. Jane had to phone Mrs Gurzky and cancel the piano lesson.

They left the squirrel in the car to rummage in the attic for a coffin suitable for a small rodent.

'I know we have a shoe box in here somewhere,' Jane said, trying to bring some normality back into her voice.

But the search resulted in only one possibility, a flat gift box from Tie Rack. They would have to squash the corpse to fit it in, Jane said.

'Perhaps it should lie in the ground without a coffin? Just like other dead animals?'

'No-o!' Julie sobbed.

Jane had to remind herself that she was grown up and mustn't let go and collapse, kicking and screaming, on the floorboards. In the end, she persuaded Julie that a decorative plant pot with cotton wool on the bottom would be right.

Greg arrived while they were unlocking the tool shed to get the spade. When he pointed out that it wouldn't be in the shed but was leaning against the wall near the patio door – as always – she snarled at him.

'So why have a fucking shed, then?'

It was so typical of Greg to turn up on the scene once the hardest part was over. Now all they had to do was to conduct a small burial ceremony for a dead squirrel.

Later, when a hole had been dug under the copper beech in the back garden and all three of them were standing by the graveside, she felt that Greg was being infuriating on purpose.

'You give the oration since you're the writer.'

Greg knew very well how much it annoyed her when people assumed that writers would be thrilled to deliver a spontaneous speech and, anyway, were especially gifted in that line.

Julie held the plant pot tight and looked from Greg to Jane and then back again. Greg sighed a little.

'All right,' he said and then, of course, spoke beautifully about the squirrel's brief life and its tiny squirrel heart, adding light touches of irony and sweet references to familiar ones like Snipp and Snapp, all done with such subtlety that Julie kept nodding agreement. So easy for him, who hadn't seen the silly little beast flapping on its ruined limbs.

After supper, Greg pulled his jacket on and said he was going over to Tom's. They were going to watch a film about Alaska.

'But I'm leaving early tomorrow morning, remember?'

'We'll meet up in the morning before you leave.'

'Before four-thirty?'

'Then we'd better say goodbye now.'

He leant over her to kiss her and she turned her cheek to him.

The whole squirrel performance had left her irritated and anxious, feelings that stayed with her all evening as she prepared for her talk at the Newberry seminar, packed the suitcase and went through a bundle of school handouts that Julie had kindly remembered to pull out of her schoolbag at a quarter past nine. When Julie – three quarters of an hour later and still not in her pyjamas – followed her into the bathroom and stood behind her insisting that she needed help with varnishing her nails because tomorrow, in the social studies lesson, she was part of a presentation on women's suffrage, Jane was too fed up to mention the flawed logic of this – or to say no. She snatched the varnish bottle from Julie's hand and pushed her against the washstand. When she had done the nails on the left hand, she said between her teeth:

'Next.'

But Julie was staring absently into the mirror.

'Julie!'

'Sure.'

She gripped the girl's right wrist hard and started on the thumbnail. Her movements grew brisker, and more determined. When she was ready to start on the ring finger, Julie cautiously freed her hand and said in a small voice, that was enough. It was fine like that.

D URING THE ENTIRE THIRD DAY in the mountains, Jane had nothing to look at except Ulf's rucksack and muscular legs. He walked through the mist guided by a compass. She was a three-year-old trailing after a cross grown-up.

They put the tent up in streaming rain. She held the sheets down against the gusts of wind while Ulf attached the guys to the tent pegs. He had made no new attempts to get close to her and barely uttered a word or two all day. Then, inside the tent, he suddenly said something nice.

'Jane, we're quite different people, you and I. But we share this: we are in the middle of a windy wasteland far from people. In a figurative sense as well.'

Then he produced a plastic bottle from somewhere and poured liquid from it into two small, metal cups.

'I remember from the plane that you like whisky,' he said.

'If I had known what we had to look forward to, I would've walked faster.'

She had trudged along behind Ulf and popped pills as if they were off to a wilderness rave party. Valium didn't seem to do much for her anymore.

'Jane,' he said without looking at her, and then shook his head slowly. Now he was either about to explain or admit something.

'Ulf,' she said in the same tone of voice.

He put the cup down on the groundsheet but kept holding on to it.

'You realize, don't you, that you must face up to things? That you can't go on like this in the long run?'

She held out her cup.

'With this cold…' He hesitated while he poured her more whisky, so she completed his sentence.

'…somehow resigned approach to life.'

'That's exactly what I was going to say.'

The wind tore at the top sheet and made the layers of the tent slap against each other.

'Do you refuse to let yourself think about them?'

'No,' she replied. 'I refuse to let myself begin to forget them.'

It was getting dark quickly now. Ulf's face, full of shadows, looked handsome. Ulf was not so bad. She had met only a few people who were actually evil. People were like characters in novels, beautiful in their fragile inadequacy. Using whatever weapons at hand, they fought to join history for a while without screwing things up too much, and always failed somehow.

'But you mustn't forget yourself.'

That, too, was a fine thing to say.

It made her think of their first day up the mountain, when they had crossed a sunken area where the low, sage-like shrubs grew so densely that their leaves formed a smooth surface of matte silver. Ulf was up to his waist after taking just one step off the path. She stood still and followed him with her eyes as he moved about through the undergrowth like an animal. The sun was warming the moisture on the leaves, creating a sphere of whispering light around him. He clambered back onto the path, sniffing at something he held in his hand and then handed over to her. It was a tuft of wool, light and soft. She could just sense its presence on the palm of her hand. Three or four black hairs were mixed with the wool. The hairs were so thick she could roll them between her thumb and index finger.

'Guard hairs,' Ulf told her. 'The white down is the inner layer. Musk oxen let the shrubs pull some of it off in the spring so they don't die of overheating in the summer. Isn't that great?'

His eyes had been shining with naked, childish enthusiasm but she had just shrugged.

Ulf drank a last slug of whisky and started to look around the tent.

'I guess we'd better have something to eat,' he said.

She slowly raised her hand, placed it on his. She had a vision of disappearing into somewhere strange, to force a feeling to emerge, a sensation powerful enough to dampen down all others. Like self-harm. He turned her hand over, squeezed it, began to stroke her palm with his index finger.

When Jane had decided to screw Ray Dechamps for the first time, they had been in the basement room in his parents' place and David Lee Roth, played at max volume, was coming through from upstairs where Ray's brother was partying with his friends. It had dawned on her just how tricky it would be to do this with her critical mind engaged, rather than abandoning all thought and clawing Ray's back while he banged away for roughly as long as the guitar solo.

Afterwards, when they were lying together on top of the sleeping bags in the dense darkness, Ulf's breathing sounded exaggerated, too heavy, as if after some sporting feat. She was cold but her clothes had ended up on the far side of Ulf. She felt like an envelope that had once contained an important document but had been reused for some other, insignificant purpose.

Ulf turned over and put his arm on her breasts. As she was lying on her back they had flattened so he had to grapple to get a good handful.

'How was it for you?'

Oh, Christ.

She sat up but his hand followed her like an animal looking for warmth, and she had to lift it away before bending over him to grab her clothes.

Ulf fired up the primus stove. The heat intensified the smell of armpits and damp wool. Streaks of rainwater ran down the outside of the tent like oil in a greasy frying pan. They sat in silence at opposite ends of the tent and ate freeze-dried curried stew. Then Ulf broke the silence. As if time had stood still inside his head, he followed up what they had talked about the day before:

'That great, superior entity of yours? Or is it a place? Is it where souls go?'

She had been considering if she shouldn't tell him that she was done with this trip, and would prefer to back out. But it felt like admitting defeat.

'The physicist deliberately didn't use the word *soul*. He only spoke of *awareness*.'

'Smart,' Ulf remarked.

She so did not need to speak about that TED Talks lecture. Not any more. She was angry with herself for mentioning it.

Tom Belotti had sent the link to the web page and she had been watching the lecture over and over again for three days. Tom had meant well. And he was the one who had found her. The door had been left open and two stove burners left on. His first thought was that she had killed herself. When he discovered her sitting in the study in front of the screen, his fear turned to rage that made his neck flare red. But he had taken her broken soul home with him to his kitchen and tried to patch her up with Vladlena's help.

When she told them that she planned to go to Norway, Vladlena had said something in Russian.

'What did she say, Tom?'

And Tom had replied, with a sigh, 'That you remind her of an animal that leaves the herd in order to die alone.'

Vladlena had punched him on the shoulder.

'But that *is* what you said!'

'Yes. Not go, Jane,' Vladlena told her.

'Listen, this guy surely thought the point was that it should be possible to meet those you loved and missed in some form or another? That in the greater whole, you can meet again?' Ulf asked.

'I recommend you listen to his lecture,' Jane said.

'Sorry. But that thought has nothing to offer except false reassurance.'

To refute the idea seemed to mean something positive to Ulf.

'I think you should consider a different line of thought, Jane. To think that your sense of loss can be understood as nothing more or less – like everything else – than atoms and molecules. Electrochemical signals, endlessly fired off.'

Ulf moved and knelt in front of the stove to shut the gas feed off. The wheezing ended and the tent filled with a stillness that laid everything to waste.

She didn't know what made her continue. 'It's the last mystery for science.'

'What is?'

'Life and death.'

'What, have you found stuff online about that, too?'

He folded the gas stove's supports before putting it away in a small container. Then Ulf got his evening routine underway: he lay down on his back and began pulling off one woollen sock. She clenched her jaw. His thigh was level with her eyes.

'We have a pretty good idea of what life is,' he said with a slight effort.

Then he straightened out again, placed the first sock on his chest and folded it slowly and methodically.

'We can introduce an electric current into a mixture of appropriate chemicals and create elements of organic life.'

He groaned as he reached for his other foot. Possibly, this was to impress her by showing that he could get his socks off.

She longed for Greg as someone who is suffocating longs for air.

Ulf took out his nasal spray and shot a dose up first one nostril, then the other.

'And we can end the process in an analogous way,' he said through a rather blocked nose. 'Mass doesn't disappear after death. And there is no evidence for consciousness being anything other than the sum of neural functions that shape our perceptions of the world.'

'Fuck you.'

'The thing is...' He was pointing at her with the nasal spray. 'You people believe that we're after something when we tell you these things. But the facts we uncover are in no way charged with meaning. Not by us, anyway. They are just facts.'

She wondered about Ulf's motives. Was he trying to toughen her up by telling her harsh truths? Or was he furious because his penis hadn't taken her straight into seventh heaven? She turned away from him and pulled the sleeping bag over the back of her head.

'I simply tell you the way things are. All you can do, Jane...'

In the moment he placed his hand where her shoulder was under the sleeping bag, she knew what he would say and realized that her reaction would be impossible to control.

'... is to let time do its healing work.'

'Go to hell.' The words came out in a low growl, as if from deep down a hole in the ground. 'Go to hell!' She was shaking inside the sleeping bag. 'I hate you. I hate you and your simpleminded cod philosophy and your crummy social skills and your shrunken little dick.' That last bit came out in a shrieking wail. Then she collapsed on the sleeping mat, her muscles contracting twitchily and her tongue growing thick inside her mouth.

In the morning, he had gone.

'AT THE DEEPEST LEVEL, my novels deal with the way we see ourselves reflected in the eyes of others while remaining fundamentally alone, and how we always long to become something more than just one being, more than a solitary brain inside an isolated organism.'

'Would you agree that this longing is given a religious dimension in your books?'

'Yes. Isn't that what religion is, simply put? A fusion of our tendency to wish to be part of a greater entity and to yearn for meaning. What I am trying to say is there is only one contemporary and also widely accepted answer to the question about the meaning of life, which is that life is sufficiently meaningful in itself. It is easy to see why this last line of defence is often articulated as a demand or a duty. We are obliged to respect and protect life, so also to recognize the worth of one's own and others' existence. It's one way of putting it.'

'But surely interactions between individuals are also important in your books? And this offers us hope, wouldn't you agree?'

'And yet, how impossible it seems.'

'How is that?'

'There are so many fools out there.'

'Ha ha.'

'If only everyone had been like Jane Ashland.'

'Indeed, yes… ha ha. Many of your protagonists are religious. Are you a believer?'

'No, I'm not, but I think the characters I write about end up believing because they discover their limitations… that is, they become disillusioned. And then they turn to God.'

'My impression is that you have always been well known at university level, in creative writing schools and among people who write for and read literary magazines. Is that right? A writers' writer, in a sense? Would you agree?'

'Well, yes. It's a compliment, in a way. But then, maybe not.'

'Now, though, with *The Age of Plenitude*, things have really… gone your way? As a journalist and a mother of two, I can't help wondering how you find time for everything. You know, what with the writing and…'

'And writing?'

'You teach as well, don't you?'

'I have a good husband. Unlike you, I don't have two children. Only one, and she is growing up fast now.'

'How old is…?'

'Her name is Julie, and she is eleven.'

'And your husband?'

'Greg.'

'What does having a supportive family mean to you?'

'Oh.'

'Did the question sound stupid? Weekly magazine style?'

'Not at all, it's fine. Julie and Greg are my life. The rest is fiction.'

TO SEE THEM. In the shop, the park, a playground, at a distance. A certain way of running, or how a child pushes her hair behind her ear. The same sweater. Listening for someone who isn't there, who has disappeared. At night, in the house, in your head. The inexplicable physical pains, the burning feeling of clothes against your skin that makes you rip them all off and stand naked in the bedroom. Climbing over the cemetery fence in the middle of the night because it is not possible to wait until they unlock the gate in the morning. Feeling hostile to everyone who grows older, somehow undeservedly. Feeling hostile towards everyone who is alive, yourself as well. Screaming in the car – people passing you in the next lane think you're singing!

Hating someone on TV who talks about grieving with dignity. Hating TV. Hating the word *accept*. Hating everything that carries on regardless, indefatigably. Hating all those who avoid you as if you were infectious. Hating all those who don't avoid you but fail to understand. Hating the spring, the flowers that dare to flourish.

THINKING BACK, the odd thing about creative writing studies was the fact that it was forbidden to write about pure accidents. She had instructed each new batch of expectant students: no accidents. Using literary power-language that seemed odd in retrospect, she had used the phrase *Deus ex machina* – God from outside the machine, a narrative trick that introduces an inconsequential or manufactured element into a story in order to solve a problem; an arbitrary turning point, unrelated to the traits of the characters and to the motivations you were meant to write about: pride, desire, egoism.

If students nonetheless produced pieces of writing where unexpected but fateful events occurred, she would explain that they had got stuck with the original storyline and picked a facile escape route, adding that, anyway, the solution was inherently unconvincing. Then she told them to write something different that would come across as more believable.

In other words, she wanted the students to write about an unreal world. Outside fiction, conditionality is a basic aspect of life. Generally, it is what people struggle with, at least when they are not fighting each other: If only I had more money... If I build this barrier tall enough... If I keep my head down and say the right things...

And then, with no permission, without respect or consideration, it hits you: the untreatable oesophageal cancer, the fire in the fuse cupboard, the armed, methamphetamine-maddened burglar who rambled along to your open bedroom window rather than your neighbour's, the winter blizzard that dumped tons of snow on the substandard roof of the sports arena.

Conditionality creates the irreducible gap between the world as you wish it to be and what it actually is: a place ill suited to creatures in search of meaning.

S HE LACES UP HER BOOTS. They have Vibram soles and
a layered construction which provides insulation but is also
uniquely breathable. You can't possibly die if you wear them.
She keeps the clothes in her rucksack but discards everything
else. Including the water bottle, because it was so long since
she felt thirsty. She tries to stop shivering and put the sleeping
bag back into its cover, but it's like trying to manipulate it with
a fist of part-thawed fish fingers. Then, she stands in the icy
rain and shakes and clings to one of the tent poles through
the thin top sheet and won't let go. The anorak hood is tied
around her head and she can see a tuft of hair sticking out and
dripping rain down the collar. Her breath smells of ammonia.
She recognizes it from the anorexic girl she shared a desk with
during biology lessons in high school.

She ought to have every qualification in the book for grasp-
ing what it would mean to Dorothy and Robert if she were
to die here. But the thought of them mourning her is still
irritating. Ulf was right. What gets to her is that her parents
will regard their emotions as meaningful in ways that have
no relationship whatever to the world she observes now, a
world that, quite unknowingly, is about to kill her – the wind,
the endless rocks, the air saturated with water molecules and

reflecting light at a wavelength that the human eye perceives as white.

She counts to nine, closes her left eye and nods politely to *the* stone, as one must in order to be safe when one passes it. Then she counts again, going down this time, and sets out with her neck bent. For each step she takes, new surroundings seem to be put in place, new shapes emerge out of the whiteness. Or, rather, more of the same. Unending ground-down stones on damp black peat, like a cobbled route unrolling in front of her.

Her idea was to work out a direction from the sky and walk straight ahead but a compass was the one thing she didn't buy before the hike. Always something, isn't there? She is pretty sure that the sun rises in the east and sets in the west. Her watch tells her it's eight o'clock but it is a Seiko that winds itself when one's arm swings, something her arm hasn't done for several days. Greg gave it to her on her thirtieth birthday. She wonders if she shouldn't take it off and leave it in some very visible place because it's so valuable.

Once, she asked a student who did parachute jumping what it felt like to fall through a cloud. His answer disappointed her: he said there was no sudden transition between the cloud and the blue sky.

You've done roughly the same on the ground, he said. *Just imagine wandering into a very low, very large fog bank.*

If she tries to think like that, it also becomes possible to believe there is something outside the cloud. But it's exhausting. She encounters some large boulders and has to walk around them. It is impossible to stick to a set direction.

She checks her watch. Now it says twelve o'clock but the brightest place is not right above her. Her steps create sodden echoes that make her look over her shoulder. She tries to speed up and walk more lightly but that's worse still. There's a sucking sound every time she lifts her heels. She can hear her own quick breathing while she wades through clumps of rushes that reach her hips. The water is seeping over the tops of her boots.

Then a mound appears some way away, a place where she can stand on dry ground. But she gets close to the mound faster than she expected and realizes that it is no more than a bump, just about large enough for the soles of two boots. She bends like a tightrope walker and, suddenly, she sees a light ahead of her. A searchlight, a head torch, perhaps the fluorescent glow of a rescue helicopter light. She splashes through the wet moorland, running towards the light that spreads and becomes stronger the closer she gets.

Just a few more steps and she sees it: it is the orange tent. A sentence comes to mind. She might have written it herself or perhaps read it somewhere or perhaps it has occurred to her at this moment.

There is a component of deprivation that is similar to starvation: a physical sensation of hollowness.

A WOMAN LOVES A MAN very much, he loves her very much, they cannot imagine a life without each other and, even though it is not said aloud or even clearly formulated in their thoughts, they take the fact that they have found each other and love each other and have created a good life together – the fact that love, after all, does exist – as proof that life as a whole has a hidden but beautiful pattern, that there is an inner order to the apparent chaos of the world around them, a lofty intention behind everything.

But these are their very last words to each other; this is how the two lovers say farewell:

'But Tom has been waiting for that DVD for ages. It's the one about the guy who builds himself a log cabin, yeah? And lives alone in Alaska?'

'Sure. You do what you like.'

B EFORE THE COURT HEARING began, she had made a
decision: she would meet the defendant's eyes as often as
possible. That her gaze would be reciprocated was something
she had not taken into account. The first time she stood face
to face with Scott Myers, outside Court 1A in Dane County
Courthouse during the chaotic moments just before the hearing
was due to start, he either pressed his chin against the narrow
blue tie he had obviously borrowed, and mumbled something
to his defence lawyer, or else used his superior height to stare
placidly at a point above her head. When the doors opened,
his lawyer escorted the client swiftly inside. They were followed
by the defendant's father, a man with a greying crew cut and
arms that stretched the seams of his blazer, who pushed Myers
from behind with his large hand, as if covering his son's back
in some kind of forward sporting move.

Scott Myers kept his eyes fixed on a point above hers during
his statement to the effect that he turned down the right to a
pretrial plea – there was no point in denying that he had com-
mitted the offence. It was all over before Jane had managed to
catch his piggy blue eyes. She had seen these eyes many times
on the web pages of the Green Bay Packers. Scott Myers was
a tackle in the reserve team. He was twenty-four years old,

six foot five tall and weighed in at three hundred pounds. He showed no signs of remorse.

Outside the courthouse, when Jane was standing on the steps with Robert and Dorothy, Scott Myers's father had come over to her.

'We pray for you, just as much as we pray for our son. I can't hope that you will forgive him. We hope that God will.'

She noticed that her body weight increasingly rested on Robert, she felt his arm support her, then almost slacken before it held her up again.

'What we're doing now, we do because it's our duty. Because he is our son. He has a right to defend himself.'

Scott Myers's father said all this as if preparing to lead troops into battle. He held his hands together just in front of his stomach. Only his red-rimmed eyes and the way he twisted a large gold ring round and round on his finger gave away that he was speaking from a bottomless depth. Jane would on several occasions come to wish that he was on her side.

Going home in the car Dorothy said, 'I understand that you couldn't bear to answer him,' which almost certainly meant the opposite. The catastrophic consequences of the accident had not penetrated into the barricaded, light-shy core of Dorothy's mind, so she actually felt that Jane had been impolite.

'I somehow couldn't breathe, Mom,' she explained.

For the duration of the court case, Jane was unable to distinguish clearly between fantasy and reality. She kept a thin notebook in her handbag – she had torn out half the pages and thrown them away because they had been used for notes on a novel – and wrote down information that had seemed important at the time, or that she had been told was important. The notes were unsystematic. One page contained a detailed description of the jury selection process, even including which day of the week it usually took place. It was followed by an almost entirely blank area devoted to a single word.

Ravens.

On the next page, written in letters that grew larger and larger:

That I write this down means...

The sentence ended there and the next two pages were empty until the entry of a date and a time and the words:

Jane A will make a victim impact statement. You will not be asked to do anything else.

Underneath, her name, scratched repeatedly in the same place until the pen had torn the paper.

She perceived her mind as a smooth black surface made from a material capable of registering a particle storm of impressions. In the evenings, lying in bed at home or in her parents' house or in Tom and Vladlena's guest room, she tried to visualize the defendant's bull neck, round red cheeks and small goatee beard. She recalled the TV interview with one of the sheriff's officers wearing a gold-braided cap and a hi-vis vest: he stood near the incident site and described the chain of events for a professionally appalled reporter from NBC. And she thought about the home page of the legal firm handling the defence, with its crass advertisement: *Not all lawyers are used to the thrill of victory after an unconditional discharge. We'll get you off the hook!*

Then, she might feel another tightening of the airways, a few seconds of increased pulse rate, a pang of recognizable emotion, like a tattered little banner blowing in the wind at the far horizon beyond a desolate battlefield.

Myers's defence neither apologized for his action nor attempted to modify his account. It wasn't that kind of case. Both sides went in for plea bargaining. Myers would admit to all the essential elements in the prosecution's case, but charges would not be pursued for minor breaches of law – such as leaving the scene of the accident. The prosecution wanted the case to be briskly concluded, without shades of doubt or pending options for appeal. As for Myers, any agreement would imply a reduced term of punishment. What such an outcome implied for Jane was obviously questionable. Her father held the not uncommon view that plea bargaining in cases such as this was typical of a legal system that was rotten to the core. Others have argued that if justice was seen to be done swiftly and in a satisfactory way, both parties would have the best prospect of moving on. As far as Jane was concerned, the first opinion was uninteresting and the second one so naïve that she briefly recalled what it felt like to laugh.

Regardless, the judge quashed the proposal and the case got underway. The prosecution's version of the events was identical to what she had been told by the sheriff's department.

Scott Myers, Aaron Harlan, a former teammate, and Harlan's girlfriend, Nicole Cason, had gone out together to a local bar, the Red Shed. According to Cason, called as a witness for the prosecution, Myers had drunk between three and six alcoholic drinks. She was certain it had been at least three because they had taken turns to buy the first rounds and she remembered having had just enough in cash to pay for the Long Island Iced Teas for Myers and Harlan, and a low-alcohol beer for herself – the bar did not accept credit cards. During the last hour before they left the Red Shed, Myers and Harlan played table football while Nicole sat in a booth chatting to an old friend. She saw Myers pass by three times with a beer in each hand, on his way from the counter to the corner with the games table. This made her assume that Myers might have consumed a total of six alcoholic drinks.

Around ten o'clock, Harlan got into a fight with another customer, an acquaintance from the time when he had been playing with the Wisconsin Badgers, the university team. Myers joined in the quarrel and became so loud that the female bouncer asked him to leave. Nicole Cason drove Myers and Harlan to the latter's apartment in Darbo-Worthington. The plan was that Myers would stay the night. Nicole went home directly because the atmosphere in the car had become too much *like a guys' night out*.

Once at Harlan's place, Myers started drinking beers and tequila shots. Over the course of the evening, several other guests came and went. When Myers and Harlan were on their own again, they shared a gram of cocaine that Harlan had acquired the night before. In the police interrogation, Harlan had only been able to state how much cocaine he had bought and what they drank, as everything else had gone from his memory. The time when Myers had suddenly made up his mind to leave Harlan's apartment had been determined from an incoherent text message sent by Harlan to Nicole Cason, in which he joked that he was so out of it, he couldn't find Myers in his two-roomed apartment.

When the police asked Myers if he was a habitual cocaine user, he said he wasn't, but *I had to do it now because we've got to be clean by June.* At this point, the prosecution explained that the National Football League carried out regular anti-doping checks to reveal usage of performance-enhancing drugs, but tested for intoxicants only once a year.

Scott Myers could not recall the reason why he, at around eight in the morning, went down to start up his white four-door Dodge Ram 2500 and drove off on East Washington Avenue. Four blocks east of the Wisconsin State Capitol, a truck driver called 911 after having spotted Myers's pickup racing along at high speed with two wheels on the planted median strip. An incident of dangerous driving had been recorded by the emergency services but had not been followed up with an immediate intervention.

Grounds for compensation, Jane's lawyer had whispered at that point.

Myers carried on westwards. At the intersection of Washington Street and Regent Street, he drove through the red light and hit a dark-grey saloon car belonging to Gregory Ashland, the driver, who was killed instantly. The shift-working assistant at a gas station on the opposite side of the railway tracks crossing Washington Avenue heard a noise she at first understood to be a loud explosion. She had assumed a train might be involved. She took the first aid kit that had been lying unused under the counter for years and ran outside to find the scene of the incident. She passed by the smashed sedan car because, as she told the sheriff's officer, she *couldn't bear the thought of what might be inside* and went to the white Dodge, which had been less damaged. She saw that the driver's cab was empty and returned to the first wrecked car, where she discovered eleven-year-old Julie Ashland in the back seat, squashed and immobilized.

Later, Jane couldn't remember the return journey from the seminar in Chicago.

A bewildered man had been blocking the entrance under the neon sign of the Emergency Department. As Jane squeezed past him, he had exclaimed *God is with you*, and the smell of his yellow teeth would come back to her for days afterwards. Several people in the reception area kept saying her name and talking to her as she sped through the hospital corridors like a corpuscle rushing through the bloodstream.

They had taped a pink, transparent tube to Julie's forehead and strips of the same tape, spotted with yellow pus, went across the ridge of her nose and down her cheek, where they met and crossed more strips holding the respirator tube in place to the left of her front teeth, which gleamed faintly in the narrow crack between her lips.

No. Please.

Jane noticed that someone was holding her arm in a gentle, painful grip just above her elbow. She didn't want the supportive hand because it confirmed that all this was true, that it really was Julie lying there, her lustrous, violet eyelids closed and her hair looking oddly dull, glued to her head on one side and fanned

out over the pillow on the other. Julie's eyebrows and her pale
lips still formed perfect arcs whose symmetry was emphasized
by the criss-crossing tape stuck all over her face by people Jane
had never met.

A blanket had been pulled right up to Julie's chin. Beneath
the dark folds, Jane sensed the presence of something she was
not meant to see, something broken, aching, packaged in a
still wet cast. Julie's right hand lay on top of the cover. The
fingers were lined up along the edge of the bed and the palm
turned upwards. An IV tube went up her arm to somewhere.
At the edge of Jane's field of vision, pale beings still hovered,
apparently understanding what went on in Jane's mind and
wordlessly telling her what to do: *Hold her hand.* Jane did. She
had felt its surprising weight before when she had held her
sleeping daughter's hand and, with a terrible chill spreading
between her shoulder blades, imagined precisely a moment
such as this.

She hadn't been there when it happened. Facing fear alone
had been Julie's last experience. If she had been conscious after
the accident, she might have called out to Greg but received
no answer. Jane leant close to Julie's ear on the side that wasn't
covered in tape. Tears stuck to her cheek and hairline, and when
she tried to wipe them off with the back of her hand, Julie's
head fell sideways a little.

No, it's impossible to tell if Julie can sense anything, but it is
good that you speak to her. After all, you never know... though,
to be completely honest... but of course that is always the way
when something has happened to your own child, anyone you
are fond of, really, you shouldn't wait to say...

So Jane tensed whatever muscles would obey commands and tried to whisper that she was so sorry for all the times when she had been too strict, or hadn't listened or had disappointed Julie, for she must know that she was always in Jane's mind, never out of her thoughts regardless of what she was doing, and that Jane couldn't imagine a life without her, and then bad conscience struck her because Julie shouldn't leave this world being worried about anything. Once more, she put her cheek against Julie's and hugged her, noticing how different the girl felt, and all the time, her mind swung between feeling that she was observing someone else's unfolding story and an infernally lucid perception of her own skull, enclosing her brain in a noisy, blood-red space.

Julie's body shook momentarily and the small spasm travelled up through Jane's arm.

'Julie?' Jane pressed the girl's hand hard, rocked it gently.

'Is this because she can hear me?'

'Sure... it could be.'

This was a lie, Jane realized.

She examined Julie's hand. The nails on the thumb and index finger were red, but the other three nails so pale that the white arcs at the torn cuticles were almost invisible.

The same thought recurred roughly every ten seconds: it ought to be possible to wind back time, to remake the end of the story because the definitive moment was just a moment and surely should be much easier to reverse than a long chain of cause and effect. This childish notion emerged and was rejected. Over and over again.

Without turning round, Jane asked if anyone had any nail varnish. No one answered.

From some distant place, she heard her own voice.

'In my bag, maybe in the waiting room... I don't know.'

'Don't worry. We'll find it.'

Six months later, she woke in the dark. She didn't know if it was early in the morning or late at night. There was a smile on her face when she woke, a fool's smile that lasted for the few seconds it took her to realize what was what. Then she had to start her breathing practice. These are my toes, I can curl them. Breathe out. Breathe in. These are my legs, they're tensing now. Upwards next, muscle by muscle.

She connected the charger to her mobile phone and waited until it showed the time of day. Four missed calls, one from her father and three from an unknown number. Sitting on the edge of the bed, she tried to remember how it used to feel before when you had had three unknown missed calls. Then her phone rang. The display showed the same number.

The man at the other end introduced himself as the prison chaplain at the Jackson Correctional Institute.

'I have tried to reach you at the university because I knew you had been working there. But you're not there any more, is that right? But the lady who took my call, she might be called Ellen? She told me that you were going away – or?'

The prison chaplain seemed to speak in questions and sounded like a seventeen-year-old. He said that Scott Myers had tried to commit suicide twice. Jane couldn't cope with holding the phone to her ear just then. The small, boxed-in voice continued to speak into the mattress. A gap between the curtains let in a shaft of blue light that swept the room and read it like the beam of a scanner: naked thighs spreading on top of a crumpled sheet, steely reflections from cutlery on top of a pile of plates, bundles of clothes, scrunched-up papers like trembling small animals taken by surprise.

She shifted position, picked up the phone and carried on listening to the voice. The chaplain had another question on his mind.

'Perhaps this is too much to ask? I'm not even putting the request as a preliminary question. I simply pass it on.'

Jane longed for a feeling she could do something with.

'He is very anxious to talk to you. Naturally, I will be present.'

Her voice grew out of the darkness. 'I'll do it if I can see him alone.'

'No problem at all, this isn't a high-security institution.'

The following Tuesday, Jane parked by the side of the road near a tall blue-painted water tower a little way from the prison, and waited there while the shadow of the tower moved across the car and into the edge of the forest.

The visiting area was a café run by the prison inmates. Jane's cup of coffee was presumably charged to Scott Myers's account. Myers ordered nothing for himself. Jane sat opposite him at a picnic table outside the café. Between them on the table lay a key on a loop of white string. Myers had grown paler but also bigger. As if he had been to a training camp, Jane suggested. That extra weight must be an advantage on the field.

'I got sixteen years, Mrs Ashland. I will be forty-one when they let me out.'

One year older than Jane was at the time.

'They tell me you've been trying to hang yourself.'

He nodded slowly.

'Is it the slip knot you can't get right?'

Myers searched her face and eyes for a sign of humour. Jane knew he would find nothing. Other people served as mirrors and, in their blank faces, she saw reflections of her own baffling lack of expression. There was something wrong about the fit between what she said and what she looked like, a disconnect that upset people profoundly. Deep down, they felt impelled to exclude her from the flock. Jane knew she was close to losing her already tenuous grasp of how to be human.

'It wouldn't have been so difficult at home in the garage but they take everything away from you here,' Myers said.

At a neighbouring table, a Latin American family nearly filled the quota of six visitors. Two teenage daughters picked unenthusiastically at a casserole dish and responded in single syllables when their mother urged them to join in the conversation. A little boy had climbed up onto the lap of the prisoner and was hitting his chest with his fists. The sky above was wide open, contradicting the idea that one place should be shut off from another.

Jane put the coffee cup down and fixed her eyes on the clay-like dregs.

'Where do I come into this?'

'I wondered if you could forgive me, Mrs Ashland.'

'Ms.'

'What?'

'Ms Ashland. I am a widow. Besides, it is usually regarded as sexist to define a woman by her marital status.'

'Oh. Sorry.' Myers held out his hands.

He had no idea what she was on about.

'So, you believe it would be helpful if I forgave you?'

Myers raised his large hands to his face and kneaded his cheeks and his greasy forehead.

'It might make some things easier for me,' he said.

He was large and sheepish. Jane thought he was a beast harbouring all kinds of lusts, imagined him grunting on the football field and making coarse comments about the cheerleaders. Somewhere in the back of her mind, she wanted to think he had violated Julie.

He placed his large hands on the table and pushed the key around in little circles.

'I see. You feel that it's my job to make things easier for you?'

'No, Miss Ashland.'

Myers kept looking over his shoulder. There was nothing to see except a soda machine against a cement wall. She registered suddenly that he was trembling inside his green overall.

'I can't feel free, if you see what I mean, not free for *real*, but free inside my head. It's not about being locked up here. But I'm scared all the time that I'll go crazy.'

'Join the club.' Said in a low snarl.

'I didn't mean it like that, Miss Ashland.'

'Ms!' A noise like a snake. 'The *s* is sounded. It's not the same as *Miss*.'

'Yeah, sorry.'

Myers turned his head towards the drinks machine again.

'What's up?' Jane asked.

He quickly turned back to face her.

'Why do you keep looking over there?'

'I don't know, Ms Ashland.' He started to fiddle with the key again. 'But I think it would be easier to feel remorse properly and really take my punishment if I don't go sick in the head. If I managed to think the right things. You see, she's there all the time. With me.'

'Who is?'

'Your daughter.'

The Latino family was being told off; Jane heard the guard go on about hands being visible. When the guard turned his back to them, one of the teenage girls did something that made the whole family laugh quietly until the little boy burst out laughing too.

'What about Greg? My husband? Do you keep thinking about him?'

'I don't know, Ms Ashland. No, I don't. Not as much, anyway. Sorry. I am sorry about that. You see, it's like I see her all the time. She's lying there.'

'Julie?'

'Yes.'

'Do you have a problem with saying her name?'

'I don't know. Maybe I haven't said it ever before. I feel bad about that, Ms Ashland.'

'Can you stop saying *Ms Ashland* in every fucking sentence?'

'Yes.' Tears were beginning to well up in his eyes.

'Don't cry!' Jane said. She got up and stood with her hands on the table. The guard slowly looked their way.

'Sorry, Ms Ashland.' Myers swallowed and clenched his jaw muscles and then looked the other way when he could no longer hold it back. Small sobs kept escaping.

'Stop it!' Jane hissed.

Shameful memories made her turn away. She remembered the times she had treated Julie like this and then forbidden her to cry. Like the mid-morning playground session in Olin Park, when Julie had fallen from the climbing frame but Jane hadn't seen it happen and thought the crying was just attention-seeking.

Oh god, these burning cheeks. How they triggered pangs of anger. She wanted to make him lick the ground. He was as stupid and innocent as a bull calf. She could make him do anything. And it struck Jane that the evil in her mind now exceeded whatever had been in his at the moment when he killed Julie.

'So, if I forgive you, you won't hang yourself?'

Myers slumped in the seat, his reddened face sagging between his massive shoulders. As he began to speak to her his eyes rolled upwards, but when his gaze surfaced it cracked and dissolved into thin air. It was similar to his courtroom behaviour but not quite the same.

'There are these things inside my head that I don't get... but I'm not really crazy. They say it's because I can't sleep. Like soldiers, they've found it out in research. But if you said you didn't hate me then I could remember that every time I think about...'

'Julie?'

'Yes. Like, instead of. Because I think about her almost all the time. That's why I'm training hard.'

Jane was approaching a boundary. She hadn't uttered so many consecutive words for a long time. The visiting time must be almost over. She was going to check the time on her watch, but it was of course in a locker at the security gate, together with her wallet.

'Can you say it, Ms Ashland?'

It came out at once: 'I forgive you.'

Myers was picking at the key again.

'What's the matter?' Jane asked.

'It didn't sound as if you meant it.'

'I don't mean anything I say, Scott.'

She had addressed him by his name. Why had she used his name?

'I open my mouth and sounds come out. Mostly, I try to say the things people want to hear. I forgive you, I forgive you, I forgive you.'

Myers was twisting uneasily in his seat. Then he rubbed his face again.

'You want me to say whatever will make your head work properly. There's a system built into your mind that makes you want to stay alive. The system asks me to help you. Perhaps I can. But how much is the built-in system worth? What are you worth?'

He looked at her with the eyes of an animal one is about to kill.

'Please, Ms Ashland, there are so many hours in here.'

'There are just as many outside.'

Jane rose. As she started walking around the table, he also got up and came towards her. The guard's hand went up to something in his belt. And then Scott Myers put his arms round her and hugged her tight. A large, soft little kid.

Jane heard the guard say: 'Five seconds, Myers.'

She noticed that he nodded over her shoulder, and sensed his breath and the smell of his body, stale and boyish, and automatically began to stroke his back as you would with somebody else's child, a little one who had fallen over and hurt himself in the playground when the parents were not around and you would comfort the child because that is what you have to do, which makes you realize that without feeling anything, it is possible to imitate how it used to be done.

THERE'S SOMETHING GOING ON OUTSIDE. It sounds like a heavy object being pulled through the heather. She unravels her arms from the sleeping bag, like a brittle insect. Next, the legs. Now she is on all fours, gathering strength in the glowing light that filters into the tent. Once the zip is down, she sees the moon shining. Only torn-off rags of the fog hang on to the slope, the rest is gone.

She crawls outside and attempts to get upright. She stands, with flashing in her eyes, rocks from side to side, draws the cold air into her lungs. The mountains are there again. A faint, red sheen glows at the far horizon but the cold has stretched the sky until it turned white, leaving only small moth holes that let out the ancient light of eternity.

Now that the air has cleared, she discovers that the tent has been erected on a raised bit of ground next to a marked path. In the moonlight, the cairns show up like lit lamps. Below, she sees the wide vein of silver that is the main road. Two cars move smoothly in the valley with a discreet shushing sound that she can, more or less, distinguish from the blood rushing through her ears. She sees the railway line. The electricity poles along it look like scorched tree trunks after a forest fire. Ulf had taken for granted that she would find her way back. In more ways than one, they were back to where they started.

She realizes what woke her and counts fourteen of them moving slowly as a group over a low ridge behind the tent. Long, ragged fur almost covers their hooves and conceals the swinging gait of the grazing animals. They are traversing the landscape as if on rails, with their muzzles buried in the heather.

An attack of cramp makes Jane bend over. She stands for a long time with her hands on her knees. Then, gradually, she straightens up and lets everything that is not moonlit and cold pass through her mind untouched, before she starts walking with long, weightless steps towards the animals.

PUSHKIN PRESS

Pushkin Press was founded in 1997, and publishes novels, essays, memoirs, children's books—everything from timeless classics to the urgent and contemporary.

Our books represent exciting, high-quality writing from around the world: we publish some of the twentieth century's most widely acclaimed, brilliant authors such as Stefan Zweig, Marcel Aymé, Teffi, Antal Szerb, Gaito Gazdanov and Yasushi Inoue, as well as compelling and award-winning contemporary writers, including Andrés Neuman, Edith Pearlman, Eka Kurniawan, Ayelet Gundar-Goshen and Chigozie Obioma.

Pushkin Press publishes the world's best stories, to be read and read again. To discover more, visit www.pushkinpress.com.

THE SPECTRE OF ALEXANDER WOLF
GAITO GAZDANOV

'A mesmerising work of literature' Antony Beevor

SUMMER BEFORE THE DARK
VOLKER WEIDERMANN

'For such a slim book to convey with such poignancy the extinction of a generation of "Great Europeans" is a triumph' *Sunday Telegraph*

MESSAGES FROM A LOST WORLD
STEFAN ZWEIG

'At a time of monetary crisis and political disorder… Zweig's celebration of the brotherhood of peoples reminds us that there is another way' *The Nation*

THE EVENINGS
GERARD REVE

'Not only a masterpiece but a cornerstone manqué of modern European literature' Tim Parks, *Guardian*

BINOCULAR VISION
EDITH PEARLMAN

'A genius of the short story' Mark Lawson, *Guardian*

IN THE BEGINNING WAS THE SEA
TOMÁS GONZÁLEZ

'Smoothly intriguing narrative, with its touches of sinister,
Patricia Highsmith-like menace' *Irish Times*

BEWARE OF PITY
STEFAN ZWEIG

'Zweig's fictional masterpiece' *Guardian*

THE ENCOUNTER
PETRU POPESCU

'A book that suggests new ways of looking at the world
and our place within it' *Sunday Telegraph*

WAKE UP, SIR!
JONATHAN AMES

'The novel is extremely funny but it is also sad and
poignant, and almost incredibly clever' *Guardian*

THE WORLD OF YESTERDAY
STEFAN ZWEIG

'*The World of Yesterday* is one of the greatest memoirs of the twentieth
century, as perfect in its evocation of the world Zweig loved, as it is
in its portrayal of how that world was destroyed' David Hare

WAKING LIONS
AYELET GUNDAR-GOSHEN

'A literary thriller that is used as a vehicle to explore big
moral issues. I loved everything about it' *Daily Mail*

FOR A LITTLE WHILE
RICK BASS

'Bass is, hands down, a master of the short form, creating in a few pages
a natural world of mythic proportions' *New York Times Book Review*